Navajo Rock

Buck Heeley and Scott Beaumont have grown up together in the small town of Navajo Rock, Arizona. John Clayton envies their long friendship, but his attempts to humiliate Buck backfire. Resentful and jealous, John plots a public retaliation. Unfortunately, his actions lead to a terrible accident, and Buck and Scott are forced to flee from their homes and families.

Peter Clayton swears revenge on them and vows to hunt them down. Buck and Scott are on their own and their friendship is tested to extremes as they fight to survive in the dry Navajo country.

Will they find justice in the face of hatred?

Navajo Rock

GILLIAN F. TAYLOR

A Black Horse Western

ROBERT HALE · LONDON

Typeset by
Derek Doyle & Associates, Liverpool.
Printed and bound in Great Britain by
Antony Rowe Limited, Wiltshire

ONE

The bell over the door jangled flatly.

'Hiya, Buck. It's a for-real shame about your ma.'

Buck Heeley turned around from stacking tins of pressed beef on the shelves of the family's store. He'd guessed the customers were cowhands from the rattle of their spurs, but he could have done without seeing John Clayton and his cronies. John sounded sincere enough but his freckled face was split with a grin. Mrs Heeley had died suddenly from coughing sickness just two months ago. The adobe house and store seemed quiet and empty without her warm presence and Buck was missing his mother more than he could have imagined.

'What do you want?' he asked curtly.

'Why, it's pay-day,' John Clayton said cheerfully. 'Me an' the Whangdoodle boys are in town to have us a blowout.' He threw an arm around Abe Johnson's shoulders.

'That's so.' Billy Hargreaves backed him up.

Buck wasn't surprised to see Billy Hargreaves and

Abe Johnson with the ranch owner's son. Buck and John Clayton had known each other since childhood, when John had been the new boy in town and had tried to steal the friendship of Scott, the preacher's son. Buck and Scott's friendship had been too strong for him to break but the childish resentments and jealousies had lingered on, even though both were in their twenties now. Whenever John Clayton came to Navajo Rock, he still made a point of showing off his friends to Buck.

John Clayton took a few steps forward and leaned against the counter, grinning up at Buck. The two were much the same build, both being tall and wiry, but were very different in colouring. John Clayton had curly blond hair to go with his freckles and blue eyes. Buck had dark brown hair and darkly tanned skin, but the real give-away was his eyes. They were the same, impenetrable black eyes of his mother and his Navajo grandmother. He stared silently at John, making the cowhand speak first.

'Well, I guess you'll not be coming to the cantina tonight for some fun with the boys,' John remarked. 'I expect you'll be thinking about your ma being in the Happy Hunting Ground. And I'm sure that's where she is,' he added piously.

For a moment, Buck was on the verge of telling him that his mother had attended Preacher George's church regularly until being buried there, and that Navajo didn't believe in an afterlife anyway, but he held his silence.

John waited for some kind of an answer to his teasing but when Buck remained apparently impassive, he stood up straight. 'I want a sack of Bull Durham,' he ordered briskly.

'We don't have any.'

'You always do!'

'We don't now. We don't have anything you want.'

John Clayton gaped for a moment before he understood that Buck didn't intend to sell him anything. 'You've got to sell it to me,' he insisted, leaning over the counter to see the shelf where he knew the tobacco was kept. 'I can see some there.'

'I'm not selling you any.'

Clayton's face flushed; he wasn't used to being denied his wishes by anyone other than his father. He fumbled some coins from his waistcoat pocket on to the wooden counter. 'There see. Now you've got to sell me some tobacco.'

Buck still didn't move. 'I don't have to sell anything to anyone I don't want to.'

Heeley's was the general store for the whole town. It carried hardware, guns, groceries, clothes and practically all the things a cowhand wanted. The only other stores in town were the feed store, the saddle-maker's and Miss Winter's dry-goods store, which catered principally for the female trade. If John Clayton couldn't get his tobacco in Heeley's, he couldn't buy any elsewhere.

'I'll buy the smokes for you,' Billy Hargreaves offered, digging into the hip pocket of his striped woollen trousers.

'No thanks, *amigo*,' John said swiftly. He was sure that Buck would sell Billy the tobacco, which would be even more humiliating.

'Come back next month,' Buck told him. 'You can buy what you like then.'

'Why, I'll make you pay for that, squaw boy,' John exclaimed furiously, using his own private name for Buck Heeley in his temper. 'I'll tell my father.'

Anger flashed in Buck's dark eyes. 'Your father can take his trade elsewhere if he doesn't like this place,' he said.

There was no other general store within fifty miles of the Whangdoodle. Peter Clayton was as hot-headed as his son but the cost and inconvenience of sending elsewhere for the things he needed for his large ranch made a withdrawal of his trade impractical. John Clayton knew it as well as Buck did.

'You ain't going to get away with treating me like this, you half-breed,' he snarled. 'You got no right to come down high and mighty on no one.' He stormed away from the counter, his friends following belatedly. The door slammed behind him, setting the bell jangling.

Buck rubbed his hand across his eyes, his heart tight with anger and grief. Quick, impulsive steps carried him across the store to gaze out at the bluffs and sky in the distance. He leaned his forehead against the cool of the expensive glass windows that had been shipped in especially last year. The tightness passed and his breathing began to ease as he fixed his eyes on the pinkish-red landscape under the intense blue sky.

Heeley's General Store was at the north end of town and there was nothing to interrupt Buck's view to the bluff that gave the little town its name. From this side of the wind-carved rock, its edge looked rather like the profile of an Indian. When Tom Heeley had opened his trading post thirty years ago, it had got known as the Navajo Rock store. As the town grew up around the store and the spring it relied on, the town gradually took the name Navajo Rock itself. In spite of being so small, it still had a sheriff's office and a Wells, Fargo office with a stage once a week. There were a few *Anglos* and more were moving in, but most of the local people were Mexican.

This north-east part of Arizona was empty and huge, vast spaces of tan, grey and pink with sandstone outcroppings and tumbled piles of harder rock that had fallen and shattered into untidy fragments on the landscape. It was the land of room enough and time, as the Navajo said. Buck's tension drained away as he let the space surround him. Glancing down the street, he could see John Clayton's bay horse waiting in front of the cantina. Buck sighed and turned back into the store.

'Move over, Bandit.' Buck pushed against the black's shoulder.

The horse snorted softly but moved over in the stall, giving Buck enough room to groom his shoulder. Most folks around town said that Buck had no more sense than a seam squirrel, to keep a stallion as his riding horse. Bandit was a true black horse with a white stripe on his face that divided in two at the top, rather like a streak of lightning. It was an appropriate marking, Buck felt, because Bandit was very fast.

Buck planned to win a few more races with Bandit this summer and then to earn some money covering mares. Peter Clayton had offered two hundred dollars for Bandit last year but Buck had no intention of selling.

Buck pushed the body-brush with long, firm strokes, leaning his weight against the horse's powerful shoulder. Bandit's summer coat gleamed like glossy satin already but Buck kept working. The stallion stood calmly, enjoying the attention. Buck was nearly done when he heard his father calling.

'I won't be a minute,' he yelled back.

'Now!'

Buck put the brush away and crossed the yard to the store, brushing horse hairs off his tan shirt as he went.

Buck's youngest sister, Mae, was in the kitchen at the back of the store building, fixing lunch. She gave him a sympathetic look as he went through, making him wonder what was up. In the store itself, his father was waiting alongside another man. Buck smiled briefly at his dry, leathery father, before realizing that the other man was Peter Clayton.

'Howdy,' he said politely. A quick glance showed that Pa was angry.

'Clayton tells me you've banned his son from this store.' Heeley waited for a good answer.

'I didn't like his language,' Buck answered.

Clayton scowled. 'All cowpokes get a little wild on pay-day; you got to know that.'

'I do.' Buck fell silent again, watching Clayton through inscrutable eyes. He let the rancher simmer for a moment before continuing. 'I don't mind cuss words, unless there's a lady in the store. It was the way he spoke about my ma . . . mother.'

All his life, Buck had referred to his mother as 'Ma'. Since her death, many of the superstitions Buck had learned from her Navajo relatives had come to the fore, not least that it was bad luck to mention the name of a dead person.

'What did he say?' Heeley asked his son.

'He called her a squaw and said she was in the Happy Hunting Ground.' Buck repeated the words with distaste.

Peter Clayton tried to gloss over the insults. 'Why, I'm sure John didn't mean no real harm by that. Of course, it was unkind of him to speak like that so soon after your sad loss. I sometimes think my boy don't have no more manners than a mule. But you were never ashamed of Mrs Heeley's family, were you?'

Tom Heeley had loved his half-Navajo wife without shame. He had even given shelter to her brother and his family for five years when other Navajo had been forced on to the reservation at Bosque Redondo. 'I know an insult when I hear one,' he retorted. 'I'm not ashamed of my wife's family, but some people reckon I ought to be.'

'And I don't cotton to being called "squaw boy" or "half-breed",' Buck put in. 'Half-breed isn't even accurate.'

Peter Clayton found himself faced by two angry men. The rancher was an older version of his son but with grey dulling the yellow tones of his blond hair.

He wore a brown suit-vest over his white shirt, and a string tie. His cuff links and watch chain were gold and he wore a silver-and-turquoise Navajo-made belt buckle. Not surprisingly, Peter and John Clayton had similar opinions on Indians and their place around white folks. Peter Clayton responded just as his son had.

'You got no right to ban John from this store,' he stormed, glaring at Buck.

'My son is a partner in the business,' Heeley answered. 'He can ban anyone he likes and I certainly stand by him.'

'The ban was only till next pay-day,' Buck said. 'And it was only John.' He meant that he hadn't banned the rancher or any of his other men.

Peter Clayton thought Buck was being dismissive of his son. 'You can't ban my son from something any *peon* can do,' he exclaimed. He glared at the two Heeleys, his blue eyes bright with anger. Neither of them responded. 'Well, I'll spread word of how you treated me,' Clayton threatened. 'Iffen all the ranchers stop using this store, you'll see the difference. We'll bring someone in and set up a store of our own, if we have to.' He turned his back and left, leaving the bell ringing over the door.

Buck sighed. 'Sorry to bring that down on you, Pa.'

Tom Heeley clapped his son on the shoulder. 'Sancha and Johnson won't back him. A month from now Clayton and his boy will be grumbling but they'll be back in here for their goods.'

'I guess so.' Buck shoved his hands in his pockets.

'They need us and we need them,' Heeley said philosophically. 'There's no reason to stop taking a man's money, just because he's a louse.'

Buck grinned suddenly. 'All right. I'm taking Bandit out now. I'll be back for lunch.' He left the store, whistling, and saddled up the black stallion. When he was ready, Buck swung easily into the deep saddle and rode out on the north trail. He rode well clear of the cemetery beside the whitewashed church, not even glancing at the newest gravestone. Graves made him shudder and he couldn't understand why people went to kneel beside holes where corpses and bones lay. The church was soon behind him though as the stallion climbed the trail on to the dry mesa. Buck's temper eased as he rode and his thoughts turned to more pleasant things. The free movements of the horse beneath him reminded him of the races and *fiesta* to be held the following weekend. And from thinking of the *fiesta* he was soon thinking of Juana, and was happy again.

Juana felt warm and soft as Buck danced with her in the fire-lit evening. Dances in Navajo Rock were held on the open ground between the church of San Paolo and Domingues Sancha's town house. The music was alternatively Spanish and *Anglo*, to suit the available musicians and the dancers. The dance ground was bright with coloured paper lanterns and bonfires, while the fitful breeze brought the smells of charcoal and hot tortillas. Juana was looking her best in a deep-red dress that set off her complexion and bright smile. She was of medium height and nicely plump, all curls and curves as she danced. Buck held her tightly for the swings, enjoying the soft rustle of the petticoats under her flounced dress.

When the song finished, Buck led her over to where Scott was standing with their drinks. Scott Beaumont was Buck's best friend and had been bringing all kinds of mayhem and scrapes into his life for years. He was Preacher George's eldest son and worked as the teacher when he wasn't helping with the local round-ups or having fun.

Some folk reckoned that Scott had altogether too much fun for a teacher, but he was good at his job and always managed to stay just on the right side of propriety, so he kept up his happy life. He was twenty-four, a couple of years younger than Buck, and chose to batch at the tiny teacher's house behind the school rather than living at home with his parents and three younger sisters. He even looked more like a cowhand than a teacher; sturdy and muscular, his pugnacious face so tanned that the freckles were barely visible. His hair always seemed slightly too long and was a mass of orange corkscrews that no amount of bay rum or grease had ever tamed.

'On with the dance!' Scott declaimed as Buck and Juana approached. 'Let joy be unconfined: no sleep till morn, when Youth and Pleasure meet to chase the glowing hours with flying feet.'

'Byron,' Buck answered promptly. It had been a game between them for years. Scott had a remarkable memory for poetry and books and challenged himself to find a quotation for every occasion. Buck attempted to guess the source and mentally awarded himself double points if he correctly remembered the writer and Scott couldn't.

'What does that mean?' Juana asked, a touch suspiciously.

'It's about young people like us having a good time at a dance,' Buck told her.

'I see.' Juana smiled admiringly at Scott, causing Buck a sudden twinge of jealousy.

'Buck. Did you hear me?'

Buck realized that Juana was looking at him anxiously; he must have missed something. 'Er . . . not really,' he confessed.

Juana shook her head. 'I asked if you wanted to go eat.'

'Sure, sounds like a great idea.'

Sheriff Millard came to join them while they were eating. He was a tall and angular man, with thinning, sandy hair that he always hid under a white Stetson. Between chewing on a chicken leg and drinking his root beer, he asked after Buck's family.

'Doing swell,' Buck answered. 'Laura's finding little Annie a handful, now she can run.' Laura was one of his two married sisters.

The conversation turned to family talk until it was interrupted by the clamour of horses being ridden fast along the street. The riders were whooping and yelling as they charged down the street in a tight bunch. In the light from the bonfires, Buck saw John Clayton leading the pack. He watched silently as the cowhands pulled up outside the cantina and dismounted, their laughter rising above the dance music.

'I hope they don't take too much moonshine on board before they come looking for a dance,' Millard said.

' "Drink no longer water, but use a little wine for thy stomach's sake and thine often infirmities",' Scott quoted, gazing reverently at his own glass of beer.

For a moment, Buck thought that the sheriff was about to start a Bible-quoting match with the preacher's son, but Millard apparently thought better of it.

'The Good Book says a little wine, not a skinful of tarantula juice,' Millard said sternly.

Scott grinned, unabashed. When the next song started, he made an exaggerated low bow to Juana. 'Would the beautiful lady dance with me, *por favor*?'

Juana smiled. 'Just once. Because you ask nicely.'

Buck watched them go, sipping at his tequila. He thought of Juana as his girl but she didn't seem to realize how serious he was about her. She had already danced with two other young men this evening. When he'd asked her about it, she'd said it was bad manners for a girl to spend all night with only one man and had gone to sit with her family for a while. Buck had never yet got up enough courage to defy the sternly watchful eye of Juana's mamma.

Lost in his thoughts, Buck started when someone tapped him on the shoulder. It was Sukie, the oldest of Scott's three younger sisters. She was a pretty girl with an attractively snub nose dusted with summer freckles. Thick chestnut hair was wound into a braid on the back of her head, but a few locks had escaped their pins and waved softly around her face as she studied Buck with her bright brown eyes. Her eyes and hair were set off by a golden-yellow dress, well made but plainer than would be worn by other girls of nineteen.

'Hello,' Buck said politely. 'Enjoying yourself?'

'Yes, thank you.' She glanced at her brother, who was whirling Juana around energetically. 'Don't you mind him dancing with Juana?' she said hopefully.

'Why should I?' Buck teased. 'She's only another woman.'

'I'll tell her you said that!' Sukie exclaimed.

Buck laughed with Sukie, half-regretting the comment. He couldn't help noticing how close she was to him; her elbow gently brushed his side. 'Have you seen Mae?'

'She's around somewhere.' Sukie gestured vaguely at the crowd.

'Has she had many dances yet?' Buck tried gossip as a distraction.

'A few.' Sukie grimaced. 'Jimmy Millbank came and asked her and she didn't dare refuse. I ran and hid before he could ask me too.' Her face said what she thought of the Rafter J cowhand.

Buck sympathized, but was distracted by seeing Scott and Juana approaching as the dance ended. 'Have you finished with her?' he called to his friend.

'Yep. You're welcome to her,' Scott answered casually. He belied his words by giving Juana a scandalous kiss on the cheek.

She threw both men a haughty look and walked off to join her family. Buck glowered at Scott, who shrugged. Buck thumped him on the shoulder and wished he'd had the nerve to kiss Juana.

The dance was still going strong at midnight. Children were heaped in sleepy, blanketed piles where the older people could keep an eye on them. Buck was slightly drunk; Scott rather more so. They leaned against a table, eating peach pie during a break in the dancing. The air was still warm and lively with conversation and merriment.

'Man did eat angel's food,' Scott quoted, savouring his slice of pie.

'That's the Bible,' Buck answered. 'And this is Mae's pie.'

'Then your sister is an angel. Can I marry her?'

'Don't ask me, ask her. On second thoughts, no you can't. If she gets married, Pa and I will have to do our own cooking.'

Scott put on a sorrowful expression. 'Then you would understand the hardships in my life; making my own coffee. You know how lousy my coffee is. . . .'

His clowning was interrupted by a shout. 'Hey, *mestizo!*'

Buck turned at the sudden call. John Clayton was ten feet away, his eyes sullen. He was also wearing a gun. Billy and Abe were standing behind him; Billy looked uneasy but Abe was grinning foolishly and holding a whiskey jar.

The silence between stretched out. Buck could feel Scott's restlessness but his friend said nothing. It was Clayton who gave way first.

'Well, 'breed? Are you goin' to let me back in your two-bit store?'

Buck answered calmly enough. 'Not till pay-day, like you were told.'

'That's not a healthy attitude to be taking. You're asking for trigger-talk.' John Clayton shifted stance, his right hand dropping closer to the Colt.

TWO

Buck said nothing, simply stared back at John coldly. He was pretty sure that Clayton had more sense than to start a shooting-match in the middle of a dance.

Clayton waited, aware of the people around watching him and his friends at his back.

'Come on, squaw boy; how much do I have to cack you? Are you as yellow as your Navajo cousins?' he challenged.

Buck grabbed Scott's arm as his friend stepped forward. People further away were still talking but those nearer had stopped. They were watching; watching John Clayton calling him a coward.

'You're plumb drunk,' Buck answered. 'I don't fight with drunks.'

'Yellow!' shouted Clayton. 'You're yellow!'

'He's as yellow as c-c-custard,' taunted Abe Johnson, who stammered slightly. He waved his stone whiskey jar in the air.

'Hold up there.' Sheriff Millard spoke firmly and clearly as he advanced across the dance ground to

John Clayton, the white Stetson pulled low over his eyes.

'You bill out of this,' Clayton told him. His hand moved away from the gun butt.

'This is my business,' the sheriff answered. He glanced momentarily at Buck, before glaring at Clayton from under the brim of his hat. 'This was a peaceable shindig afore you showed up. I'm telling you to take yourself off home, right now.'

'It's a free dance,' Clayton protested.

'An' I'm the sheriff,' Millard pointed out. 'If you don't get on your hoss now, I'll lock you all in the hogpen overnight for being drunk, and your father'll have to bail you out.'

Still glaring at the sheriff, Clayton took a step backwards. He paused, switching his stare to Buck. 'I'll make you fight, squaw boy. See iffen I don't.' Then he spun round and left, barging past the friends who trailed after him.

Buck let out a deep breath, conscious of others still looking at him. He wondered what Juana and her family had made of the exchange. At his side, Scott relaxed.

'You did the right thing there, boy,' Sheriff Millard said. He came across to them, a slight grin on his long face. 'You did good to keep your temper while he was saying things like that.'

'I don't want to fight him,' Buck said clearly. 'Folks like that aren't worth the fighting.'

'That's right,' Millard agreed. He glanced at Scott. 'You listen to what he says; turn the other cheek.'

'I'll try.' Scott was grinning as he promised. Buck's

family had been more welcoming to him than his had to Buck. From boyhood, the two friends had spent far more time at Buck's house, and Scott had learned to love Buck's family as much as his own. He felt Clayton's insults as keenly as his friend did.

The level of talk was swelling again, much of it about himself, Buck guessed. In the background, the band started playing again and the dancing went on.

Tom Heeley said nothing to his son beyond a word of praise for his restraint. 'One day, those Claytons will go too far,' he said. Buck busied himself putting the black stallion into harder training for the Fourth of July races. Long rides at a steady walk or trot put the finishing touches to the horse's powerful muscles. By the time the holiday dawned, Bandit was a fit handful of a horse.

Buck tightened his hold on the reins slightly as Bandit cantered on the spot. The stallion's neck was arched and his thick tail held high, as he tittupped down the street. He was a splendid sight and Buck sat proudly as they approached the crowds around the ploughed oval of dirt that served as a race track. Bandit lifted his head and gave a trumpeting challenge to the other horses. Folks turned and made way when they saw Buck approaching on his excitable horse.

'You keep that black demon well away from anyone,' warned McCall, the smith who had the trouble of shoeing the stallion every month.

Buck saw his family, his father, Mae and his two married sisters with their husbands and children. He waved cheerfully to them, still scanning the crowd for Scott. He spotted his friend's brightly marked pinto first, and nudged Bandit over to him. Buck was surprised to see that Scott was talking to his father, who gave Buck a cold look as he approached.

'I take it that you are racing today?' Preacher George asked.

'Yes, sir,' Buck answered, dismounting gracefully.

'For the sake of your mother, you should reconsider,' the preacher demanded. 'Gambling is a sin and she would not have wished you to behave in such a way.'

'My mother attended the races every year; these ones and the Navajo ones,' Buck answered defiantly. 'Are you racing?' he asked Scott.

'Yes,' Scott said stubbornly, not meeting his father's pale eyes.

Displeasure radiated from the preacher like heat from the sun. He turned on Buck, his voice stern. 'It is your pagan example that has led my son into bad ways. I urge you to turn your back on sin, before it is too late!'

Buck couldn't help recoiling from the force of the preacher's personality, but anger gave him the courage not to apologize for something he hadn't done. Preacher George had disapproved so often, of so many things that Buck and Scott had done together, that Buck found himself seething with dislike for his friend's father.

'Could you hold Bandit for me?' he asked Scott. 'I've got some business.'

'Sure,' Scott said automatically. He took the

excited stallion's reins and edged the horses away from the crowd.

Buck gave a polite nod to the preacher, and moved away. He mixed with the rest of the crowd, making wagers and taking a look at the other horses. Cowhands from the three local ranches were also in the crowd. Each ranch had a couple of entries and the men were boasting about their horses. Not surprisingly, one of the Whangdoodle's entries was John Clayton on his bay. Buck tried to avoid the rancher's son, but when he turned away from arranging a bet with Juan Olmo, he found himself face to face with John.

'Don't waste your money betting on that coffin-headed donkey,' John Clayton told Olmo, ignoring Buck altogether. 'Put it on my Bay Knight.'

'The bet is already made,' Olmo answered. 'And I am not the *hombre* to change my mind.' As Clayton turned away, Olmo winked at Buck.

With all the wagers being made, almost half an hour passed before the horses were gathered on the track. By that time, Buck's stallion was thoroughly excited. Bandit's glossy coat was patched with sweat and the stallion would not stand still, but danced continuously, snorting like a steam engine.

'Get lined up now,' called Sheriff Millard, who was acting as starter.

The horses jostled together, heads high and ears pricked as they caught excitement from their riders. A sorrel swung its quarters against Bandit. Buck saw his horse's ears flatten and he pulled on the reins, swinging his horse away before it could bite the sorrel. Bandit screamed a protest and plunged up and down on the spot, fighting his rider. Buck kicked his stallion, intent on getting it out of the crowd before he did any damage to someone else's horse. He was facing away from the others as they formed a rough line across the track.

'Go!' yelled Millard.

The other horses all leapt forward in a bunch. Bandit spun on his back legs and plunged after them, almost leaving Buck behind. By the time they reached the first turn, Bandit was hemmed in amongst a group of mid-paced runners. John Clayton's bay was a couple of lengths in front of Scott's pinto; the next runner was a couple of lengths behind that. With Bandit held up in a group, Buck tightened his reins and managed to regain some control. They stayed in the group around the first turn into the back stretch. Up ahead, John Clayton laid his quirt into the bay and urged it into a sprint. The bay responded, opening up a lead of several lengths. As the group came off the turn, the horse immediately in front of Buck ran a little wide. Bandit laid back his ears and forced his way into the narrow gap. The other horse gave way to the stallion and Buck had gained a couple of places.

Buck was inhaling fine dust with every breath. He could feel the power of his stallion beneath him as the horse ran, its thick mane whipping in the wind of its speed and stinging against Buck's hands. He kept the same position along the back straight and moved up around the far turn. The race was over two laps and John Clayton's bay was already finishing its first as Buck ended the second turn of the oval. A couple of horses fell back a little. Buck urged the stallion forward. Bandit responded eagerly but was bumped by another horse sprinting past. The stallion staggered, losing the rhythm of its strides for a couple of paces and the other horse was in front.

Buck sat tight in the deep saddle, letting his horse balance itself. They were on the inside of the track but boxed in by a liver chestnut with flashy white markings, Billy Hargreaves's horse. It was half a length ahead, its rider about level with Bandit's head. The stallion's ears flicked back as it galloped, annoyed by this obstacle. Billy had his quirt in his outside hand and was waving it steadily, stopping his horse from moving away from the stallion. They stayed like that around the turn and came once more into the back straight. Clayton's bay had the advantage of most of the back straight over Scott's pinto, which was losing ground fast. Buck was trapped to the left of the liver chestnut. He knew Bandit could run faster than the liver chestnut and would get past eventually, but he was running out of time.

'Go on,' he urged, digging his heels into the stallion's sides. Bandit pushed closer to the liver chestnut, shouldering against its quarters. The horse started to give way. Billy Hargreaves lashed it with the quirt, trying to keep it straight, but the liver chestnut was more afraid of the stallion. As it moved to the right, Billy swapped the quirt from hand to hand. He brought the quirt down in a wild stroke on his horse's shoulder. In passing, the leather lashes on the quirt slapped against Bandit's face. Most horses would have shied away or dropped back, but not the stallion. Before Buck knew what was happening, Bandit turned his head and bit a chunk from Billy's leg.

Billy yelled in pain, accidentally swerving his horse to one side. Bandit barged his way through the gap and bolted. The stallion's strides grew longer, eating up the ground now he had space to run. Buck half rose in his stirrups, letting the horse move freely beneath him. Scott had pulled his tiring horse wide so there was plenty of room to pass. Ahead, John Clayton's horse was already well into the last turn. Bandit stretched out his head and gave chase.

Buck couldn't have stopped his horse even if he had wanted to. With every long, reaching stride, Bandit got closer to the bay. John thought he had the race sewn up. The crowd was cheering madly, waving and even jumping up and down as the black stallion raced. Clayton lifted his hand from the reins to wave, thinking that the crowd was cheering him. Only when Buck was a handful of lengths behind him did he realize the danger. Clayton leaned forward and dug his spurs into his horse. The bay's stride lengthened but it had started to slow. Bandit was already at full flight as the bay gallantly tried to pick up its pace again. Bandit drew alongside and for a couple of strides, the horses were matching stride for stride. Neither rider glanced at the other, each man concentrating on his horse. The bay stretched its neck out, its nostrils flaring. Bandit surged on again, pushing his nose in front. He got a whole head clear, and then was half a length up.

Buck barely noticed the exact moment when they passed the finishing post. Only a few strides later did he sit back and try to slow his horse. Bandit fought against the restraint, shaking his head as his stride began to slow. They were half-way around the turn again before the stallion dropped to a bouncing jog. Buck turned him and found Scott alongside on the blowing pinto.

'I knew you'd beat me, but I didn't expect you to take so long about it,' Scott said, extending a hand to congratulate him.

'Got boxed in,' Buck explained briefly, accepting the handshake. They rode back to the line, where friends and family crowded around to congratulate the winner. Bandit was still excited but the effort of the run had calmed his temper somewhat. Clayton had already dismounted and handed his blowing bay horse to Abe Johnson when Buck slid from his saddle and offered his hand to the other man.

'You got a good horse,' Buck said. 'He sure put up a fine fight.'

Clayton stared coldly at Buck and turned away, ignoring the offered hand. Buck stood awkwardly for a moment, then turned his back too. The sheriff was approaching, holding the ten-dollar prize. Buck started to smile but his pleasure was interrupted when the Whangdoodle cowhand pushed between them.

'Your damned hoss bit me!' Billy Hargreaves accused. 'That critter's plumb dangerous. It didn't ought to be allowed to race.'

Millard stopped and tilted his white Stetson lower over his face. 'What's this?'

'Look at this.' Billy appealed to the crowd around them as he showed the bloody patch on his cotton trousers. Bandit had torn a flap of cloth clean away and taken a chunk of skin and muscle. 'It was your hoss,' he told Buck. 'It should be disqualified. It's for-sure dangerous.'

'You waved your quirt in his face,' Buck answered heatedly.

'We were racing! Everyone's entitled to use a quirt in the race.'

'You were keeping me boxed in so's John could win,' Buck said. 'And when I started coming past anyhow, you quirted Bandit on the head.'

Billy Hargreaves answered by punching Buck in the face. Buck just saw the blow coming and turned enough so the blow hit his cheek instead of his nose. The impact staggered him back against Bandit, who snorted and laid back his ears.

'I'll clean your plough for saying things like that!' Billy yelled, advancing to follow up. He swung again, aiming low.

Buck twisted and half blocked the punch. It hit him on the ribs, forcing him to take another step back. Sheer instinct made him step away from Bandit, but the stallion acted anyway. Neighing shrilly, Bandit reared, flailing the air with his front hoofs.

'Whoa, boy,' Buck called, immediately forgetting about the Whangdoodle cowhand. He still had hold of the stallion's reins.

The crowd around them scattered, sensibly backing away from the excited horse. Sheriff Millard caught Billy's collar and hung on to him as Buck calmed his horse.

'This's meant to be a holiday,' he warned. 'Quit fighting or you'll spend the rest of the day in the hogpen.'

Billy Hargreaves scowled but had sense enough to stand still until Buck had got the stallion under control. 'I still say Buck acted unfair,' he complained.

Buck made a grimace of exasperation. 'Your quirt hit Bandit's face. That's why he bit you. Any horse with spirit'd do the same.' There was laughter in the crowd.

'The black won,' someone called. 'No matter why he got held up, he ran the best race and won.'

Other voices agreed; Buck could see friends in the crowd nodding.

Millard considered. 'I say Bandit wins. Even though I lose ten dollars to Buck.' The second half of his pronouncement was lost in the cheering.

Buck accepted his prize money, thinking happily of all the wagers he'd be collecting soon too. More friends came and congratulated Buck as he led the black stallion back towards his stable.

'I want that black devil to cover my sorrel mare when she comes into season,' said H.P. Johnson, the other *Anglo* ranch owner.

Buck negotiated a satisfactory fee, pleased with his work. As he set off again, he spotted Billy Hargreaves and John Clayton in close discussion. They seemed to be having a disagreement, Billy demanding something and John shaking his head. Billy gestured at the still slowly bleeding wound on his leg. John

Clayton got out his pocketbook and handed over a couple of ten-dollar notes, an unsatisfied look on his freckled face. Billy took the money and limped away. Buck thought about telling the sheriff what he had seen but changed his mind. He'd still beaten Clayton anyway.

He had left the crowd behind when he heard another voice calling his name. It was Peter Clayton, John's father. The rancher waved to Buck, who halted his horse reluctantly.

'Congratulations on a fine ride,' Peter Clayton said, catching up. He patted Bandit once on the shoulder, not wishing to upset the powerful horse.

'Thank you,' Buck said a little warily. His jaw was getting stiff from being punched by Billy but he felt like a king sitting astride his horse.

'I'd like John to have won,' Peter Clayton admitted disarmingly, a wide smile on his face. 'But I have to say that the best horse won. I'm willing to pay three hundred dollars for your stallion, cash on the barrel-head.'

'Bandit's not for sale,' Buck answered, stroking the stallion's neck. The horse was calm now and seemed to be resting in the hot sun.

'All right then; I'll make it five hundred dollars,' Peter Clayton persisted. 'And any horse you choose from my remuda.' The rancher was still smiling but the warmth had gone from his expression. 'You can be sure we'd take real good care of him.'

'I'm sure,' Buck said politely. 'But he's not for sale at any price.' He saw a flash of anger in the rancher's eyes. Like his son, Peter Clayton was used to getting what he wanted. Buck tightened his hold on his reins, causing Bandit to lift his head. 'I'd best be getting back and seeing to him,' Buck said, kneeing his horse on.

The rancher had to step back as Bandit started walking. He flicked a look of admiration and envy at the horse, then forced a smile for Buck. 'Well, congratulations again,' he said.

'*Gracias.*' Buck nodded to him and rode home.

THREE

The brief fight after the horse race was soon forgotten in the holiday atmosphere. Preacher George read the Declaration of Independence aloud in the middle of the street and everyone cheered. There was dancing, drinking and feasting going on, and bunches of firecrackers being let off in the streets. Eventually, hours later, the party began to wind down. Women took the children home to bed; groups of cowhands set out on the long ride back to the ranches. Buck left a die-hard poker game in the cantina to go home. He strolled back slowly, enjoying the fresh night air. Buck took a quick look at Bandit, who was dozing peacefully in his stall, before letting himself into the back of the store building. He didn't go to bed immediately, but lit a lantern and settled in the parlour, reviewing his day as if he were telling it to his mother.

Buck took down the brown-toned framed photograph that hung over the fireplace and sat with it in a rocking chair. Pa was in the middle of the picture, looking as tough as rawhide. Beside him was Ma, dark, round and placid with her arm around her youngest daughter. At the back were himself, Lizzie and Laura, all rather self-conscious. He felt a wave of sadness as he thought of her, but it wasn't the crushing misery of the first few weeks after her death. Time passed as Buck lost himself in memories.

He was brought sharply back to the present by the crack of a gunshot from the street outside. Buck jerked, almost dropping the photograph. For a moment, he didn't know what was happening, then he could hear an indistinct singing. Buck grinned and rose, setting the picture back on its hook before leaving. As he slipped through the alley between the store and the cantina, the singing got louder. Leaning on the corner of the adobe, he watched Scott pacing a few steps back up and down the street as he sang a marching song at the top of his voice. The rendition was not too bad; Scott always sang better when he was drunk. Then Scott punctuated the verse by letting off another shot. Buck heard the thunk of the bullet striking timber not too far away.

'Hey, *amigo*.' Buck spoke before coming into view. He wandered towards his staggering friend. 'Time to quit and go to bed.'

'You want to go to bed?' Scott slurred. 'It's over there.' He pointed at the store.

'I don't want to; it's you ... oh, never mind,' Buck went on as Scott started singing again. He took hold of Scott's shoulders and tried to push him in the direction of the schoolhouse. Scott leaned heavily against him.

'I am a man, more sinned against than sinning,' Scott remarked heavily.

'Shakespeare; and I'll sin you iffen you don't get to bed, pronto,' Buck said. A sudden gleam of light from down the street caught his eye. It was the door to the sheriff's office opening. Someone came out and the door closed again. Buck pushed urgently at Scott, trying to get him to move. 'Come on, light a shuck for home,' he muttered.

Scott took a couple of steps, then stopped and tried to focus on the figure approaching them. 'Whence and what art thou, execrable shape?' he enquired loudly.

'I'm the sheriff,' came the sharp-toned reply.

Buck felt limp: too late. 'He's just going to bed.' He tried to make excuse.

'You were going to bed, not me,' Scott said helpfully. He straightened up very carefully, facing the sheriff.

'Well?' said Millard.

'I have very poor and unhappy brains for drinking . . .' Scott started.

Buck trod heavily on his friend's foot, ending the recitation in a yelp. He looked pleadingly at the sheriff. 'It's a holiday. He's good usually.'

'Good! I sometimes wonder iffen Preacher Beaumont and his wife didn't adopt that one. That red hair's plumb unnatural to his family for a start,' the sheriff said.

Scott squinted cross-eyed, trying to see the ends of his curly fringe.

'It ain't right for the son of a preacher to act like that one does,' Millard went on. 'He ought to be more like his brother, Paul, going to theology college an' all.'

'Preacher Beaumont couldn't afford to send both of them to college,' Buck pointed out. 'Scott earns his own keep.'

'And spends it all on rot-gut. He can sleep it off in the cells tonight.' The sheriff spoke firmly.

'No,' Buck said anxiously. 'That's not fair. The School Board would have to dismiss him; they couldn't have a teacher who spent the night in the pokey.'

'He should have learnt his lesson afore this.'

Buck sensed that Scott was about to speak and forestalled him by standing heavily on his foot. 'If they dismiss Scott, where are they going to find another teacher? There's no one so good as him for a couple of hundred miles out here. Your Billy-Joe would have to do with a second-class education.' Buck spoke with the inspiration of desperation.

'Hmmm.' Sheriff Millard scowled at Buck through the darkness. 'You got a point there.'

'Sure,' Buck agreed. 'You let me take him to bed now; he'll go to sleep pretty quick.'

Millard nodded, then turned and walked away briskly. Buck gave a sigh of relief, then started pushing Scott toward his house.

'You'd damn well better stay asleep,' he muttered.

'Sleep that knits up the ravelled sleave of care. The death of each day's life, sore labour's bath. . . .'

Buck let Scott ramble on as he got his friend indoors and lit a lamp. 'I hope you're going to be grateful for this in the morning,' he said, bending to pull Scott's boots off. Scott muttered disjointed poetry and Shakespeare to himself as Buck pushed him into bed and put the lamp out. Buck stood silently in the pitch darkness, listening to the mumbles turn into steady breathing. When he was sure Scott was safely asleep, he left, closing the door quietly. He couldn't help grinning; if it wasn't for Scott, there wouldn't be half as much entertaining gossip in Navajo Rock.

The air smelt warmly of baking, welcoming Scott to the kitchen of his family home. He closed the back door and kissed his ma before sitting down, away from the table. His ma was working with his youngest sisters, Ruth and Lizzie, doing the weekly bake. All three wore large aprons, made over from old clothes but newly washed and crisp with starch. The pleasant smells and general air of neatness made a welcome change from his bachelor living in the school-teacher's house. After a polite exchange of greetings, Mrs Beaumont fixed her eldest son with a stern eye.

'I heard tell you were drinking the other night.'

'I was, Ma.' Scott never lied to his mother.

'Mrs Millard told me you were firing your gun late in the night.'

'That's right.' Scott thought vaguely that surely it was only Catholics who went to confession. 'It was the Fourth of July; I was celebrating.'

'Our national day is no excuse to be drinking and bringing a bad name on yourself.'

His ma always said such things in a reasonable way. Scott suddenly felt guilty about the shame she must have felt when the sheriff's wife mentioned the incident. He stuck his hands deep into his pockets and fiddled with coins and keys. It wasn't the way his father would have tackled the subject but Scott was intent on avoiding him for as long as possible.

'Your father gave his opinion on the subject,' his ma said.

Scott wondered whether all mothers could read their children's minds. Mrs Beaumont understood her son though, and did not follow up her remark. The increasing differences between her happy-go-lucky eldest son and her stern husband disturbed her and she too thought it was better to let things lie.

'Are you getting enough to eat?' She changed her questions to more motherly concerns.

'I don't do so badly but I don't have a woman's touch at baking,' Scott answered ingeniously.

'You should get married,' Ruth suggested. 'Then you wouldn't have to come here begging.'

'I'm not begging, squirt,' Scott retorted. 'At least I earn my own keep.'

'I hear tell Buck's getting real serious about sparking Juana,' Ruth remarked.

'Now, now; gossiping is unladylike. You shouldn't speculate about grown men like your brother's friends,' her mother interrupted.

'Sukie said she wishes Juana would fall off a cliff,' Ruth said importantly.

'And you shouldn't tell on your sisters either.'

'But it's unchristian for Sukie to say that,' Ruth pointed out self-righteously.

'That's between her, your pa and God,' Mrs Beaumont finished firmly.

Ruth looked suitably crushed and went back to cutting out raisin cookies in silence.

'How's Paul? Has he written lately?' Scott asked about his brother.

His mother shook her head. 'Likely he's working too hard at his studies to write.'

'He'll make a good preacher,' Scott said affectionately. His brother had always been too meek to win his respect but at least Paul would be a gentleness and forgiveness preacher, not a hellfire and damnation one like their father.

When the baking was in the stove, Mrs Beaumont told her daughters to wash up and fix coffee. She escorted Paul into the pretty parlour and sat down. Only one of the chairs was upholstered; the rest were plain wood: Preacher George said too much comfort was a sin. Scott held the comfortable chair for his mother to sit in.

'I'm surprised it wasn't Buck Heeley you were drinking with,' she said quietly.

'Now, Ma. You know Buck hasn't been to the cantina since his ma died,' Scott said reprovingly.

His mother sighed and leaned back in the deep chair. 'She was a kind, Christian, woman and her daughters are models of good behaviour. It's a shame that Buck gets himself into scrapes.'

It occurred to Scott that the same might be said about himself and his family but he said something else. 'It was Buck kept me out of the hogpen the other night. He's a good pal, Ma.'

'I know; he's a kind-hearted young man. I cannot blame him for taking exception to what John Clayton said, but the Whangdoodle gets paid next week and there's going to be trouble. Buck just gets into things without thinking them through first and that's a flaw.'

'We are all of us flawed, Ma.'

'We have God to help us and guide our hand.'

Scott smiled at the gentle advice. 'You should be the preacher,' he said. 'You always say the right thing.'

Mrs Beaumont blushed at the unexpected praise from her difficult son. 'The Lord loves us all,' she answered.

'You don't have to work in the store today,' Tom Heeley told Buck. 'We need goods picking up from the railhead; you could do that.'

'No, Pa,' Buck answered. 'It won't make things any better. Clayton called me yellow an' if I'm not here on pay-day he'll tell everyone it's because I'm scared to face him. I'm not letting that dumb-ox who wears a ten-dollar hat on a five-cent head make out like he's better than me.'

Heeley smiled at his son's spirit. 'Go on then.'

The morning was quiet. Only a few people came in for goods and Buck sensed a slight unease about them. They seemed to keep watching the door and departed without lingering to talk. They all knew when it was pay-day on the Whangdoodle as well as he did. Buck spent most of his time on the stool behind the counter, staring blankly out of the wide windows. He was working off some of his pent-up nerves by dusting the shelves when John Clayton entered. The cowhand was on his own for once, and smirked when he saw Buck holding the old cloth rag.

'I see you're a fine hand with the woman's work,' he remarked, leaning insolently on the counter. 'Why, I'll bet you'll make someone a lovely wife.'

Buck flapped the duster, sending the dust in John's direction. 'I'm surprised you've got the nerve to come in here on your own,' he answered. 'Indian territory can be plumb dangerous.'

'What, root-digging Navajo?' John said scornfully. 'Now, Apaches, them's dangerous Indians.'

Buck scowled but held on to his temper as he moved to the back of the counter. 'What do you want, Clayton?'

John Clayton was enjoying himself; he had so rarely succeeded in annoying Buck in the past. Malicious pleasure warmed his eyes as he smiled. 'Why, I was enjoying the pleasure of your conversation,' he said, leaning both elbows on the worn, wooden counter-top. 'Us Whangdoodle boys gets all behind about what's going on in town. Which girl is it you're sparkin' now, lil' Sukie or that Messican, Juana?'

Buck wanted to swear, then grinned suddenly. 'I ain't made my mind up which one I want yet,' he bragged. 'I could have either of them. Any girl taken a shine to you?'

He knew perfectly well that John Clayton wasn't going with any of the town girls, and that his chance of meeting anyone else at the ranch was pretty remote. Five years ago, John had shown an interest in Laura, Buck's middle sister, but she'd married Tommy Weston, who worked at the livery barn. John had danced once or twice with Sukie until she'd complained very publicly about the way he trod on her feet when dancing.

John Clayton's good mood vanished abruptly. 'I'll go tell Juana's pa what you just said,' he threatened, straightening up.

Buck fought down momentary panic. 'He won't believe you,' he insisted.

'Her folks aren't keen on you anyhow,' John taunted. 'You not being a Catholic.' The taunt hit on a truth that Buck hadn't wanted to admit to himself. John saw the success of his attack and built on it.

'I just bet they got their eye on someone else for her; Olmo's son maybe. They're letting you spark with her to make him jealous. If she's had other men come calling, she'll look more of a catch when they give her to him.'

'You got no right to talk about Juana and her family like that!' Buck exclaimed.

John Clayton laughed. 'Now you're starting to look like a real mean Indian.'

At that point, Buck lost his temper altogether and simply rammed the duster he was still holding, full into Clayton's smug face. John Clayton staggered backwards, coughing, and hurled the duster into a corner.

'Why, you son-of-a-bitch! I'll pay you back for that good!' He swung around and kicked over a barrel of nails. They scattered across the floor, disappearing under boxes and shelves. As Buck scrambled across the counter, John seized a barrel of hard candy and upended that too. The colourful sweets mixed with the nails as they spread across the board floor, scattering under shelves and boxes. The nails could be picked up again, but the candy was spoiled and worthless.

'You can damn well pay cash for that lot!' Buck yelled.

'Make me!' John taunted, grabbing for a flour barrel.

Buck didn't wait to see what John was doing. He simply launched himself across the store, straight on to John's back.

FOUR

Buck grabbed John Clayton around the shoulders, staggering him across the floor. Clayton spun, smashing Buck against the other counter. Buck grunted as its edge dug into his thigh, and let go his hold. Clayton turned to face him and the two started trading blows. Buck's father was away, taking the wagon to the railhead at Gallup to pick up goods. Mae was visiting Sukie so there was no one in the store building to hear the fight.

Their fists slammed into one another. John swore breathlessly as Buck mashed his fist into John's face and split his lip.

'Goddamn you,' Clayton exclaimed, turning away. Drops of blood from his lip splattered on to the clean board floor.

Buck paused, still angry but not out of control. 'Are you willing to leave peaceably?'

Clayton stayed hunched over, breathing heavily as he glanced about. 'I don't take orders from the likes of you.' He grabbed for a pickaxe handle and swung around all in one motion.

Buck had been half-expecting another attack. Instead of backing off, he stepped close to John, getting well inside the axe handle's reach and grabbing for it. He hung on, the hickory axe-handle pinned between the two of them as they wrestled for it. The two young men were almost touching as they struggled. Buck had wiry strength but John's life on the ranch kept him fitter and stronger. After the first moments, Buck knew he couldn't hope to win through sheer strength. John Clayton grinned as he realized that he was going to pull the axe handle away. That grin was more than Buck could stand. He braced himself, then ducked his head and butted John in the face.

John Clayton cried out as Buck's head hit him on his already sore mouth. He let go his hold on the axe handle and stumbled backwards, clutching at his nose and mouth. Buck tossed the pickaxe handle into a corner and advanced on the other man. Grabbing a double handful of John's once-smart shirt, he dragged the other man to the door.

'I don't want you in here, you cur,' he hissed. Buck shouldered the door open and pulled Clayton through after himself. Tightening his grip, Buck swung round and threw John Clayton off the sidewalk and into the street. Off balance, John staggered a couple of steps and went sprawling on to the dirt.

'You got no right to come into this store and start calling me names!' Buck yelled. 'You can go tell your pappy on me if you want, like you did when you was six. I don't need my pa to fight for me. I can settle your hash on my own! Don't you come back in here unless you come to make apologies and pay for the damage you done!'

Buck paused there and looked around. Others were watching the scene with great interest. Miss Winter was in the doorway of her store opposite, Mrs Millard beside her, still clutching a skein of embroidery silk. The usual loungers around the cantina were frankly agog, grinning as they looked at John Clayton lying in the street.

John was painfully aware of the audience too. His blood-smeared face flushed red as he got to his feet. He heard the door of the store closing as Buck went back inside, but didn't look. The fury simmered within as he stalked away, tucking in his rumpled shirt and mopping the blood from his face. But even if he didn't look at them, he could hear the catcalls and the first whispers of the new story going around town. By nightfall, everyone in Navajo Rock would know that John Clayton had been literally thrown from Heeley's store. That knowledge burned.

Buck started out of his sleep later that same night. Thin moonlight filled the bedroom with eerie shadows as he lay still, his heart racing. There was a faint noise from outside, then something more distinct; the sound of a running horse just below his window. Buck hurled his sheet aside as he lunged to the open window, leaning out into the night. Someone was running away, heading out of town along the north trail. In the moonlight, all Buck could tell was that he was riding a dark horse. Pulling his head back in, Buck slid his pants on and padded barefoot to the landing.

The wooden stair-treads were rough under his bare feet as he moved slowly down, knowing just where to step so they didn't creak. The sound that had woken him must have come from the store itself but he could hear nothing now. He inhaled softly a few times but there was no smell of smoke. Buck paused behind the door, bracing himself as he listened. There was no sound. Taking the handle in his left hand, Buck shoved the door open and slipped through. Nothing. The store was silent, full of moonbeams and shadows. Sliding around to the knife cabinet, he closed his hand around the comforting weight of the largest one there. His heart was thudding steadily in his chest as he padded behind the counter, his eyes peering into every shadow.

There was nothing hiding behind the main counter. Five swift steps brought him across the open space to the hardware section. Buck circled the barrel of nails, the knife held ready in front. He still could not see anything out of place. Buck turned on the spot, aware now of a cool draught against his bare skin. He spun to face the store door but it was closed, just as it should be. Puzzled, Buck looked around until he saw the moonlight illuminating the jagged edges of the hole smashed in one of the plate-glass windows.

Fear turned to anger as Buck looked at the damage. The store windows had cost Pa a lot of hard-earned money; they had been a luxury for the whole family. Buck took three rapid steps towards the window before he felt something brush his foot. He froze, glancing down. Needles of shattered glass glimmered around his bare feet. Solid amongst them was a rock, pale scratches showing from when it had been flung through the valuable window.

By Sunday morning, the fight and the attack on the store were the main topics amongst the townsfolk gathering outside the churches. The *Anglo* community attended Preacher George's whitewashed wooden church at the north end of the town while the Mexicans attended Mass at the elaborate, stone-built church of San Paolo nearer the south end of town. The broken window had been boarded up, making the store rather gloomy inside. It matched Buck's mood as he walked to the church with his pa and Mae.

'Didn't you see who it was?' asked Matt Collins, the feed-store owner. They had stopped outside the church porch while the womenfolk straightened their bonnets and settled clothing blown awry by the desert breeze.

Buck shook his head. 'All I saw was a dark horse.'

'Could have been John Clayton on that bay,' Collins said wisely. 'I just bet it was. He looked mad enough to chew nails and spit rivets after you throwed him out of the store.' Collins grinned at the memory.

'What about Billy Hargreaves?' suggested McCall, the smith. 'He was as mad as a hornet over getting bitten in the hoss race.'

'They were both in Chavez's cantina all night,' Buck told them. 'Sheriff Millard went and asked folks this morning.' Right after finding the broken window Buck had gone to check on his stallion. Bandit had been undisturbed but before breakfast, Buck had fitted a large padlock to the stable door. 'I reckon Billy would have acted sooner, iffen he was that sore, though.'

'I just bet Clayton had something to do with it; it was mean enough for him,' Collins said, raising his hat to the sheriff and his wife as they arrived.

Polite greetings were exchanged all around before Buck spoke to the sheriff.

'Did you ride out and see Peter Clayton?' he asked.

'I did,' Millard answered, tilting his white Stetson backwards. 'John swore all which ways that he doesn't know who threw the rock.'

'He would,' grunted Tom Heeley.

'His pa raised a fuss at me for accusing his boy of doing anything so mean. He done told me I should arrest you for assaulting John, and even said you'd bust the window yourself just to make John look bad.'

Buck was astonished. 'I never even . . .'

Millard smiled thinly. 'I know you ain't like that,' he said, as the others reassured Buck that they believed him.

'Why you was so proud of them fancy windows you strutted around like a dog with two tails for a whole week after they was put in,' Collins said.

'Can you think of anyone else who might want to do either of you a meanness?' the sheriff asked Buck and his pa.

Buck wondered about how many enemies people

thought he had. 'Not a one really,' he answered, half indignantly. 'Could have been one of John's other pals. Billy was with him all night but Abe Johnson's always showing off to John.'

The sheriff read Buck's expression accurately. 'Iffen there's someone else holding a grudge about something, this is a good time for them to take it out on you. Anything bad happens to you and folks will blame John Clayton.'

'That's because John's a low-down, cheating skunk,' Buck answered firmly.

'Someday he'll push things too far and all his pa's money won't be able to get him out of the hole he's dug himself into.'

'When are you going to let him back in the store?' the sheriff asked, his expression suggesting that it had better be soon.

'When John Clayton apologizes,' Tom Heeley answered, resting one hand on his son's shoulder. 'He's got no right to come into our store and start throwing bad names around.'

Sheriff Millard nodded solemnly. 'I can't argue with that. But we can't have bad blood in the town. I don't want a feud developing.'

'Tell the Claytons that,' Buck answered, his tone barely civil.

'I already did.'

The church bell ceased its clanging and they had to hurry into church before the service began. Buck's family always sat near the front as they had been in the county longer than anyone else. Preacher George's family sat right in front. Scott looked all stiff and uncomfortable in his Sunday clothes; his corkscrew hair was already getting the better of the grease that was supposed to hold it neatly for church. The familiar sight of his friend's wayward hair put Buck in a better mood. As he settled himself next to Mae on the hard wooden bench, his thoughts turned to more pleasant things.

He was thinking of Juana when a nudge in his ribs brought him sharply back to the present. Mae was standing up and he hurried to join her. They sang a vigorous hymn, then he managed to pay some attention to Preacher George's sermon about the sin of lust. It was one of his most lively subjects, if perhaps uncannily close to some of Buck's recent thoughts. He was relieved when the sermon was over.

Buck's family stopped to speak to Preacher George's family after church. While Mae and Sukie chatted, Buck and Scott fixed up to go hunting together. The preacher interrupted them

'I haven't seen you visiting our churchyard,' he said to Buck.

'No, sir,' Buck answered, uneasily meeting the preacher's glittering eyes.

'Your sister is a fine example of a dutiful child.'

Buck glanced at Mae. His sister was naturally still dressed in mourning for their mother, but was discussing the style of Sukie's new yellow frock with keen animation. 'I pray for my mother every day,' Buck told the preacher, resentment touching his voice.

'It would be a greater sign of respect to visit her resting place,' the preacher insisted sternly.

A look of distaste and panic flickered on Buck's

face before anger took over. His grief for his mother was deep and he couldn't see that standing beside the remains of her body would make him a better son. There was no point in saying as much to Preacher George. Buck swallowed his anger and simply nodded, breaking off the conversation as soon as decently possible. Not for the first time, he felt sorry for Scott.

Buck checked over the stallion's hoofs while he waited for Scott a couple of days later. They were going out early to do some hunting before the day got too hot. Buck was all ready and had his horse tethered to the stable in the yard behind the store. He was leaning over the stallion's near fore when he heard Scott's horse arrive. He dropped Bandit's hoof, straightened up and started to turn. He just glimpsed something coming towards him, then the rope dropped over his shoulders and pulled tight.

The rope hauled him helplessly off his feet. Buck hit the ground with his shoulder and rolled, getting dust in his face. Spitting and swearing, he could hear Scott laughing at his practical joke. He managed to get half upright before the rope pulled him over again.

'This ain't funny,' he spat, rolling over. Then he realized that it wasn't Scott's laughter. Buck lunged up in a half-panicky move. It was John Clayton, sitting casually on his bay gelding with the end of the rope dallied around his saddle horn.

'You look mighty purty down there in the dust,' Clayton mocked. 'That's where you Injuns belong, isn't it?'

Buck threw his weight back against the rope but it pulled painfully tight. John Clayton was the boss's son but he did his fair share of work around the ranch and knew how to tie off a rope properly.

'You ain't got no more sense than an addle-brained calf,' Clayton said, his fair face flushed with excitement. He reined the bay horse to step back, forcing Buck to move in order to stay on his feet.

'Take this clothesline off,' Buck yelled, trying to free his arms.

John Clayton just laughed and began backing his horse towards the alley between the store and the cantina. He meant to pull Buck into the street and let everyone see him. Buck tried to dig his boot-heels into the ground and resist, but the sun-baked ground was too hard. The rope bit into his arms through the light cotton of his summer shirt. Clayton jerked him along, step by step.

'I'm gonna pay you back proper for throwing me out of that two-bit store of yourn,' Clayton told him. 'No one gets to act like that to John Clayton. What you did to me, I'm gonna do back to you, cowhand style. You're a mangey cur an' the whole town's gonna see you tied up like a no-good dog.'

He was so busy mocking Buck that he didn't hear the horse approaching from behind.

Scott took in the situation with one glance, and lost his temper completely. He kicked his pinto sharply in the ribs, so his mount lunged forward alongside Clayton's bay. The bay shied and turned just as Scott dived from his horse on to Clayton, dragging him from the saddle. They hit the ground together between the horses, rolling over and over. Scott flailed wildly, landing a blow on Clayton's ear. The horses jumped away from the struggling pair almost under their feet. A hoof caught Scott a hefty blow in the small of the back. Taken by surprise, he was knocked flat, losing his grip on Clayton.

Buck had been pulled over by the panicked bay horse. He scrambled to his knees and found the rope had gone slack. Seizing his chance, he threw the noose over his head just before the frightened bay bolted down the alley and into the street. A yell from Scott drew Buck's attention that way. Clayton scrambled to his feet and kicked Scott, aiming for his ribs.

'It's me you wanted to fight!' Buck shouted, running towards him.

Clayton turned and they met in a flurry of fists. Buck's temper was fully roused and he threw vicious punches, trying to hurt as much as possible. Clayton fought back wildly against the volley of blows. Buck hardly felt the blows he was taking in return. All his recent anger and grief was funnelled into the punches he launched at John Clayton. He just wanted to see the other man's face pulped and bloody. The rancher's son staggered backwards, trying to protect himself from Buck's fury. Scott had picked himself up and was yelling encouragement to his friend. Buck paused a moment, gasping for breath, and gathered himself. Clayton took his chance and lashed out with his foot. The boot hit Buck square on the groin. Totally unprepared, Buck crumpled in agony, unable even to cry out and helpless against Clayton's anger.

FIVE

'I've got you, you half-breed desert rat,' Clayton crowed. 'I'll make you pay for turning me out of your two-bit store and settin' your tame sheriff on me. I'll give you something to remember.' He pulled his gun out, intending to shoot the black stallion.

Scott didn't wait to see what John Clayton was aiming at. He dashed forward and kicked Clayton's hand, knocking the Colt away. The wild move left him off balance. Clayton saw Scott stagger and went straight for him; he crouched and rammed a punch right under Scott's ribs. Scott felt as though he'd been kicked by a mule. He bent over, clutching at his ribs as he gasped painfully for breath. Clayton seized the front of Scott's shirt and spun him around. He let go in time to send Scott staggering back to crash into the stable wall. Scott crumpled to the ground, still gasping painfully.

'*Que es? Que pasar?*' The sounds of the fight were attracting attention. A Mexican was peering out of his adobe not far away. Other people in neighbouring houses were waking up, wondering what the noise was.

Buck was still on his knees, bent over with the pain from Clayton's kick. Having dealt with Scott, Clayton lunged at Buck, shoving him on to his back. Buck struggled feebly as the cowhand grabbed the front of his shirt and slammed his head into the ground. Buck tried to resist, bracing his neck muscles, but the impact half-dazed him.

'You don't look so smart now,' John Clayton whooped. He hauled Buck up and slammed him against the ground again.

The back of Buck's head smacked hard against the dry ground. Coloured lights flashed in front of his eyes and he was getting dizzy. He grabbed wildly at Clayton's arms but couldn't shift him. Another stunning blow weakened him; he couldn't find the strength to lift his arms any more.

Scott finally managed to draw a deep breath again. He lifted his head and looked to see what was happening. Buck was in trouble, real trouble. Clayton rammed his head into the ground again and Buck was barely moving.

'You won't never leave me out again,' John crowed, intent only on hurting Buck as much as possible. 'I've got my own friends now and you won't show me up in front of them no more.' The old resentments spilled out of him as he slammed Buck's head against the ground again.

Scott tried to stand but his sore ribs brought him down again. He lurched forward on to hands and knees and crawled forward, cursing under his breath

Every movement brought stabs of pain from his bruised chest. He found something under his hand: it was the gun. Without thinking, Scott picked it up and shot Clayton from where he was. The rancher's son jerked violently and fell limply over Buck, pinning him.

Buck felt a tremendous weight over his chest and stomach. He opened his eyes and saw Clayton's white face, with the freckles imprinted darkly on it. Clayton stared at him from a few inches away. He tried to say something that got cut off as blood suddenly gushed from his mouth. Then his eyes glazed and he fell slack, his head dropping against Buck's shoulder. Buck lay still for a moment, dazed and bewildered. Then he suddenly realized that Clayton was dead. He pushed the body away in fright, scrambling himself clear.

'Oh, God.' The explosion of the shot had cleared Scott's head. He got to his feet and half-staggered to the body. The bullet had ripped clean through John Clayton's chest, spraying blood across the stableyard and Buck's clothing. Scott swallowed bile, sick to his stomach. All the same, he looked wildly about. No one had seen him kill Clayton but the gunshot wouldn't be ignored. Someone would come along soon.

'We've got to high-tail out of here.' Scott pulled Buck to his feet. Buck staggered and clung to his friend for support. His face was patterned with splashes of drying blood.

'Get on Bandit,' Scott told him. 'Go on.' He pushed Buck towards the restless stallion and went to catch his own horse. Luckily the pinto hadn't strayed far. Scott mounted and rode back for his friend.

Buck was on the stallion but he didn't seem capable of thinking straight. Fresh blood trickled from his mouth. Scott leaned over and took the stallion's reins, avoiding an ill-tempered snap from the horse's teeth. He kicked the pinto into a gallop and raced away to the north. Scott spared a single glance for his family home nestling in the shadow of his father's church. Tears stung in his eyes as they fled into the wild country.

It was mid-morning when Scott stopped his pinto near a stream. Both horses plunged their muzzles in and drank while Scott and Buck slid off. They staggered to the water and collapsed beside it. Buck scooped handfuls of chilly water over his face while Scott just plunged his whole head in. After cooling off they began to drink. Once their thirst had been sated, they moved away and collapsed listlessly. The only sound for a while was the horses grazing eagerly on a patch of grass, and the distant bleating of sheep.

Scott was the first to sit up. He untied his wet bandanna and wiped his face, smearing away the remains of the grime from their long ride.

'How are you?' he asked.

'Stiff as all hell,' Buck replied ill-temperedly. His muscles ached, he was still dizzy and he had a blinding headache. He glanced once at the sun and turned away, shading his face with his arm.

'You're a bit of a mess.' Scott dipped his bandanna in the creek and carefully dabbed Buck's face. Buck winced as it pressed a bruise on his cheekbone but mostly kept still. 'That's a mite better,' Scott said at last.

'*Gracias.*' Buck gingerly touched the sore spot on the back of his head. It dawned on him that he had lost his hat back in the stableyard and he didn't have anything to keep the sun out of his eyes. He sighed. 'What now?'

Scott was silent for a minute. 'Food,' he said decidedly.

'I mean about John Clayton!' Buck exclaimed. 'He's dead! I mean . . . Hell, I don't know.'

'What's done cannot be undone,' Scott quoted. 'We're both worn out. We'll think better when we've eaten chuck and rested.'

Luckily both of them had packed a few supplies for their hunting trip. The meal was a thin one of jerky and raisins, washed down with water, but it helped to restore them. They ate silently, each occupied with his own thoughts. Scott was the first to speak.

'I'm sorry I did it.'

Buck shrugged slightly. 'It was his own gun; he pulled it first.'

'But I'm the one who fired it.' Scott sounded tired. He tried to tell himself that maybe John Clayton wasn't dead, but he couldn't believe it. He could remember the mess of Clayton's chest all too clearly; the thick blood spilt on the ground. More of the same blood was dried on to Buck's tan shirt.

'Why did you do it?' Buck's voice was harsh.

'I don't know!' Scott yelled in frustration.

'You must have had some reason!'

'Maybe I was trying to save you from having your ungrateful head knocked galley-west and crooked.'

'Maybe that would have been better than being out here on the run. I don't want to be an owlhoot.'

They were both shouting, too overwrought with death and shock to think clearly.

'Why don't you go back then? I'm the one put lead in him,' Scott said.

'Because folks'll reckon I did it. I'm the one he was wrangling with!'

'Well, I'm sorry,' Scott yelled angrily.

Buck's frayed temper gave way again. He lashed out at Scott, swinging a wild punch into his friend's face. Scott punched back, getting a hit square on Buck's chin. It knocked him backwards, bringing a fresh wave of dizziness. Buck rolled away and curled up, feeling sick.

'I'm sorry!' Scott exclaimed. 'I'm sorry,' he said again as he watched his friend anxiously. 'I didn't mean to hurt you.'

Buck stayed still for a few moments until the sick feeling passed. 'I started it,' he confessed, sitting up slowly.

'It's my fault we're in this mess,' Scott said contritely. He pulled absent-mindedly at one of his corkscrew curls.

'We're both in it,' Buck answered.

The silence returned. Buck lay down again, turning his eyes to the heavens.

'What are we going to do?' He spoke to the sky.

There was another pause before an answer came.

'Let's move on.'

Buck didn't answer; he just got up and caught his black stallion.

After three days they were still indecisive and lonely. It was easy enough to keep away from other people in the vast country of bluffs and canyons. Buck's Navajo family had taught him to find water and catch small animals in even the poorest country, but they only carried equipment for a day's hunting in summer. All they had was a pocket-knife each, their rifles and canteens, a tin of sulphur matches and Scott's lariat. Leaving his horse tearing hungrily at the leaves of a cottonwood, Buck climbed a rock and lay on the stone. Its warmth was soothing and he relaxed, feeling his headache ease as he gazed into the distance, where the Chuska Mountains were hazily blue under the arching, brilliant blue of the summer sky. Scott came and lay beside him.

'We'll have to go back,' he said.

Buck just nodded slightly, filling his eyes with the space in front of him. He hadn't fully recovered from John Clayton's attack and the continuous riding was taking its toll. He had always been less talkative than Scott and his headaches made him quieter than ever.

'There's no point just running out here,' Scott went on, looking down at the rock. 'We might as well get it over with. It was an accident,' he added unconvincingly.

Buck spoke for the first time in hours. 'Uncle Billy told me to look at beautiful places and remember them. Then you have them with you wherever you are.'

Scott lifted his head to look at the high desert landscape. The soil was reddish, scattered with broken rocks and clumps of vegetation in faded greens and greys. His idea of beautiful was the lush, green Missouri country where he had been born. The desert entranced Buck as he looked at it though, points of sunlight reflected in his black, Indian eyes.

'Let's go.' Scott got to his feet and waited.

Buck turned his face to the sky for a few moments, lingering on the vastness. Then he followed Scott back.

They came back into Navajo Rock from the north. The town looked just the same: the main street, the clusters of whitewashed adobes, the colourful market stalls shaded by the cottonwood that grew next to the well. There were people on the street: friends. They stopped and stared in silence as Buck Heeley and Scott Beaumont rode slowly through the middle of town. Nothing had changed here except themselves. Buck glanced at his father's store and felt an odd sense of distance from his only home. He could see himself reflected in the one intact window and it startled him. His clothes were crumpled and he looked shabby; his slight beard was beginning to show.

The news of their arrival was travelling ahead of them. Buck and Scott rode on, ignoring the whispers and stares. They only looked away from their horses' ears when the door to the sheriff's office opened. Millard came out and leaned against the porch rail, settling his white hat firmly down as he waited. They dismounted, patting the tired horses, and stepped up on the sidewalk. Without looking, they both knew that people were gathering closer, listening.

'We've come to turn ourselves in,' Scott said.

Millard nodded. 'We had a posse out chasing you but I didn't reckon as we'd catch up to you, not out there. I'm glad you came in yourselves.' He straightened up, becoming officious. 'Buck Heeley, I'm arresting you for the murder of John Clayton. Scott Beaumont, I'm taking you in for aiding in the same killing.'

'Wait.' Scott held up his band. 'Buck didn't shoot anyone. I did. And it was self-defence.'

Millard glanced at the dried blood on Buck's shirt. 'John Clayton was after Buck, not you. Go on,' he added, pushing Scott towards the door.

The cells were beyond the office; two iron-barred cages and one small cell with solid walls. Millard opened one of the iron cages and stood back to let Buck and Scott inside. Buck settled wearily on a bunk, too numb to do anything else. Scott continued to protest as the sheriff locked the door after him.

'It was me,' he insisted. 'Clayton was whupping Buck good and I was going to help. Take a look at Buck; he's got lumps the size of plums on the back of his head. I found the gun and fired it to stop Clayton killing Buck. It was Clayton's gun; he drew iron on Buck.'

'I arrested you according to the warrants,' Millard said. 'I'll take a statement from you both later and we'll see about changing things.'

The door from the office opened as Tom Heeley

came through The sheriff moved to stop him but Buck's father simply pushed past.

'Buck?' He called through the bars to his son.

Buck sat up slowly and gazed across the cage to his father. His face was drawn as he made the effort to speak. 'I'm sorry, Pa.'

'It'll be all right,' Heeley said firmly. 'That jackass was harassing you; everyone knows that. I'll get a good law-wrangler from Phoenix or someplace to defend you.' He was pressing against the bars, getting as close to his son as he could.

'Tom.' Millard took hold of the storekeeper's arm, pulling him away. 'You go on back to your place and get Buck some fresh clothes and his washkit,' the sheriff advised kindly.

Heeley nodded, reluctant to take his eyes from his son. He took a step away then turned and called to Scott. 'I'll get Preacher George to send something for you too.'

'Thank you.' Scott had noticed his family's absence. He was grateful to Buck's father but it made him feel more isolated from his own.

Millard took Tom Heeley into the front office, closing the door on the two miserable prisoners.

News of their return rapidly spread beyond the town. Riders carried the gossip out to the ranches and to the Whangdoodle, fifteen miles from Navajo Rock. There, Peter Clayton looked out at the fresh earth over his son's grave and made swift plans. The first that Scott and Buck knew about it was in the grey light before dawn the next morning. They were jerked from sleep by a raucous rattling on the steel bars of their cell. Buck opened his eyes and blinked in the dimness.

'Wake up! Get dressed quick, 'cause you ain't got long.'

Buck half-recognized the voice yelling at him. Pushing the light sheet aside, he sat up and saw Peter Clayton and half a dozen of his men outside the cell. Scott was stirring too, mumbling under his breath about the row.

'Get up there, you half-breed murderer,' Peter Clayton called, running the big bunch of cell keys along the steel bars. The ranch owner's face was twisted with a cruel smile as he unlocked the cell door. 'Get dressed up because we're taking you to a cottonwood hoe-down. You two are the guests of honour.'

Clayton's men pushed into the cell and dragged the sleepy prisoners from their beds.

'Take a good look at that dawn,' Billy Hargreaves told Buck as he pinned the man's arms down. 'You'll be swinging by the neck afore the sun's much higher.'

SIX

Scott made a quick try for freedom. He jerked his wrist free and shoved one of the cowhands backwards against the low cot. It was Abe Johnson; he fell backwards on to the cot, arms waving. Scott straight-armed another man in the chest and lunged for the door. One of the men holding Buck drew his gun and turned. He slammed the gun hard across the back of Scott's head. Scott staggered, fetching up against the steel bars of the cell. He clung to the bars for support. The man he'd shoved aside kicked him savagely in the small of the back. Scott arched in pain and collapsed, moaning.

'Leave him alone!' Buck yelled, throwing his weight backwards and forwards in an effort to free himself from Billy Hargreaves's grip on his arms. 'You can't do this, Clayton!' he shouted, hoping that someone would hear the noise.

The sheriff and his family lived in the adobe next door. Buck didn't know it, but Millard had left the cell keys in the front office of the jailhouse. Most of his prisoners were drunks locked up overnight,

71

generally for their own safety. The sheriff had trusted his townsfolk not to try releasing Buck and Scott. He simply hadn't guessed that Peter Clayton might come looking for vengeance.

'You killed my son,' Clayton answered bitterly. He stayed outside the cell, watching as his men forced some clothing on to the prisoners. 'You'd swing anyway; I'm saving the county the cost of a trial.'

'It was self-defence,' Buck insisted as he was hustled towards the cell door. Peter Clayton stepped forward and punched Buck in the face with all the force he could muster.

'You murdered him,' Clayton hissed.

Buck's head snapped back, bouncing off someone's shoulder. Waves of pain swamped him and he could taste salty, metallic blood in his mouth. His eyes were watering so much he could barely see as they were half-carried from the jailhouse to the street. He heard hoofbeats and a warning cry from someone.

'Careful with the black devil; he's mean.'

Rough hands pushed Buck on to a horse and he settled naturally into the deep saddle. The intense pain was fading and he knew he was on Bandit. Scott's vividly marked pinto was alongside and both of them were surrounded by mounted men. A red-haired cowhand settled his lariat around Buck's arms, pinning them down. Buck recognized Oscar Crawford; he'd served him in the shop many times.

'Stop this, Oscar,' Buck pleaded with him. 'Millard won't stand for this. Clayton's just getting all of you deep into trouble.'

Oscar glared at him, his eyes startlingly blue in his red, sun-burned face. 'I liked John Clayton.' He tightened the rope.

'Lynching's murder!' Buck protested.

Abe Johnson had hold of Bandit's reins and was leading the horse across the street to the cottonwood tree by the well. Someone else was leading the pinto and the mounted men crowded around both horses, urging them on. Scott too had a lariat around his arms and chest. He tried to slide from his saddle but a rope flew through the air and settled neatly around his neck.

'Goddamn you all to hell!' he yelled, eyes blazing.

The cowhand who had thrown the rope backed his horse away. Scott shook his head futilely, his wild corkscrew curls more rumpled than ever. The noose snapped tight and his angry yells were cut off.

Buck heard the harsh choking noise Scott made and deep fear almost paralysed him. Peter Clayton was already standing under the cottonwood, supervising as his foreman tossed another rope over a branch, letting the noose dangle.

'This one's for you, Buck Heeley,' Clayton called. 'You'll be swinging just as soon as you've seen your *amigo* there stop kicking.'

Buck shuddered at the hatred in the rancher's voice. Sweat was running down his back even though the sun had barely risen and the morning was still cool. The black stallion sensed his master's fear. The horse was already on edge, being handled by strangers and now surrounded by a hostile mob. Bandit laid back his ears and jibbed, refusing to move. Abe Johnson tried to coax the stallion, knowing better than to simply pull on the reins.

'Get on with you,' urged Oscar Crawford, leaning over to slap Bandit's rump.

The black stallion lashed out with both hind feet, almost throwing Buck over his head as he kicked the horse behind. That horse wheeled away, whinnying as its rider cursed. Other horses moved away, catching the restless fear. Billy Hargreaves made an attempt to close with the stallion, forcing his reluctant mount closer. Bandit reared with a fierce, fighting scream as he pawed the air. One iron-shod hoof struck Abe Johnson in the chest, knocking him off his feet. He landed in an untidy heap, several ribs crushed by the blow. The other horses backed away, intimidated by the stallion's challenge.

Buck saw his only chance. When the stallion landed after rearing, Buck deliberately kicked him in the belly; Bandit hated being kicked behind the girth. He half-reared and went for the nearest horse, sinking his teeth into its neck. The horse squealed; and tried to pull away. Bandit whirled, almost trampling on Abe Johnson. The two men who had gone to help the injured cowhand scattered, throwing themselves clear.

Crawford had dropped his lariat when Bandit had kicked his horse and it had fallen slack. Buck managed to lift his arms and free himself from the rope even as Bandit plunged beneath him.

There was a tremendous uproar and confusion. Peter Clayton was shouting orders to his men. They were yelling at one another, fighting to control their horses and trying to keep clear of the stallion. The horses were snorting and squealing as they milled around, trying to flee from the stallion but being hauled around and quirted by their riders. One horse backed into a market stall and sent it crashing to the ground. A pole hit another horse over the quarters; thoroughly unnerved, it bolted and fled down the street in spite of its rider's efforts to stop it. Dust flew in the still morning air, half-obscuring the action. Doors and shutters were being opened in nearby adobes as the noise woke the town. Above all, came the fighting screams of the furious stallion.

Buck gathered up his horse's reins almost unnoticed in the midst of the confusion. He looked anxiously for Scott, who was still astride his pinto. Scott's arms were still pinned but the noose around his neck had fallen slack, the long end trailing on the ground amongst the men and horses.

'Get over there, boy,' Buck urged his horse. Bandit plunged sideways, tossing his head as Buck tried to exert some control. 'Get over to Splash.' Buck rode hard, using reins and legs to bring the stallion under some control again. Long habits of obedience told as the stallion high-stepped in the direction Buck wanted, still snorting piercingly. Luckily the pinto was somewhat used to Bandit's presence and was less frightened of the stallion than the other horses were. Scott saw Buck approaching and used his legs to stop the pinto moving too far away. Buck leaned precariously from his saddle to pull the loop from Scott's neck. Red marks showed on Scott's skin where the rope had bitten in.

Buck was reaching for the rope around Scott's arms when the stallion spun around and kicked a horse that had got too close behind. The saddle horn dug painfully into Buck's stomach as he lurched forward in the saddle, grabbing a handful of the stallion's thick mane for safety. The pinto jumped away, out of arm's reach.

'Stop them!' yelled Peter Clayton, his heart set on vengeance for his son. The rancher wore no gun of his own so had to take one from the holster of the man nearest to him. Clayton fired towards Buck and Scott, frightening his men's horses again and increasing the confusion.

Neither Buck nor Scott had any idea where the shot went, but they knew it was meant for them.

'Ride for it!' Buck yelled over the hubbub.

Scott rammed his heels into the pinto's sides. His horse took off with a leap and fled across the street. The end of the rope pinning Scott's arms writhed and bounced behind them. Buck turned the stallion and followed, crouching low in the saddle. He heard a couple more shots and tensed, expecting to feel pain. The stallion thundered across the street in a few strides and chased the pinto through the alley between the smithy and the sheriff's office.

From there, only the livery barn's corral lay between them and the edge of town. Bandit caught up with the pinto and Buck steered him alongside.

'Slow down,' Buck called, trying to reach the rope bouncing over the pinto's quarters.

'How?' Scott snapped. His horse's reins were

loose, flapping underfoot and his arms were still pinned to his sides.

The reins were the greatest hazard. If the pinto were to tread on the loose reins while running it would come crashing to the ground. With his arms bound, Scott would have no chance to break his fall. Buck took his reins in his left hand and closed his legs to the stallion's sides. The horse stretched his stride, his head low as he put every effort into over-taking the other horse. The earlier fury had been transmuted into the desire to run. Within a couple of strides Bandit had drawn slightly ahead so that Buck was level with the pinto's head. He leaned from the saddle again, fishing for the reins. One bounced against his outstretched fingers. Buck snapped his hand closed and straightened in the saddle. Already he was trying to slow Bandit, bringing the stallion back from the flat-out gallop.

Only when the horses had settled to a blowing jog did Buck turn to check for pursuit. There was no sign yet of anyone behind them. He leaned over to pull the rope off Scott's arms and coiled it up neatly.

'Those sons-of-bitches!' Scott's protests petered out in a dry, sore cough. He rubbed cautiously at the weals on his throat. 'The bastards,' he croaked.

'We need to get out of sight,' Buck said. He pointed to a range of pink and black rocks rising from the vast plateau that the town was built on.

They rode in silence until safely within cover and out of sight from the town. Scott rubbed at his throat now and again, his normally cheerful face drawn as he remembered the pain and fear of being choked.

The horses picked their way over rocks until Buck drew rein in a hollow.

'What now?' he asked.

Scott shook his head. 'I don't know.' He let the pinto tear up some rough grass.

'We must have made enough noise to wake the whole town. Clayton won't dare try that again or Millard will take him in too.'

'I'm not going back.'

Buck looked at his friend. 'We shouldn't run away from what we've done.'

'Damn John Clayton and damn his father!' Scott said vehemently. 'He doesn't care which of us killed John, he wanted to string both of us up. I felt that rope around my neck and I won't let it happen again!' His face was pale, the freckles standing out darkly as he spoke.

Buck fiddled with a lock of Bandit's mane. He didn't want to leave Navajo Rock but he didn't know what to do. 'We haven't got any kit with us,' he said, turning his mind to immediate matters. 'Not even a pocket-knife.'

All they had were the clothes they were wearing, their horses, the rope Buck had taken off Scott, and Scott's canteen, which had still been fastened to his saddle.

'We'll get some,' Scott said determinedly. His face it up with a sudden, wild grin. 'I bet there's hardly a man at the Whangdoodle right now. We can get there before Peter Clayton and his men and we can take what we need from there.'

Buck almost reluctantly grinned too. 'Come on

then.' They turned their horses to the south and rode.

This was the high plateau country, with the mesas of the Hopis hazily blue in the distance. The new sun flooded across the wide open land, streaking it with long shadows from every rock, ridge and bush. The reddish-pink soil glowed in the early light as the sky above became a richer and more intense blue. This had once been Navajo territory but Peter Clayton, like other white settlers, had come out here and started running his cattle on the poor ground even before the Navajo had been rounded up by the army and taken away. It was almost twenty years since the Navajo had returned to their homeland, but their reservation was small and the white settlers stayed on the lands they had grabbed. Buck's relatives had once lived in this area before being driven off. They passed an abandoned Navajo hogan as they rode towards the Whangdoodle.

'Look at that,' Buck remarked, pointing to the many-sided dwelling. 'This is a good spot to live. There's a little spring, and a patch of grazing and a wonderful view. And that's a well-built hogan.'

'Be it ever so humble, there's no place like home,' Scott answered. To him, the weather-worn hogan looked extremely humble and its location was isolated, to say the least.

'Whoever built that wouldn't have left of their own accord.'

'Perhaps he went looking for a neighbour and died of starvation on the way.' Scott's frivolous remark earned him a glare from his friend.

An hour later they came within sight of the Whangdoodle ranch buildings. They approached cautiously, using the intermittent cover of bushes and the folds of the ground to keep themselves largely out of sight. The ranch house was made of rough lumber but the bunkhouse, barn and other buildings were of adobe, in the local style. Thin smoke trickled from the ranch house chimney and a few chickens strutted out front, but there was no other sign of life. A windmill creaked in the slight breeze, pumping water into a rust-streaked tank. Buck and Scott halted at a safe distance.

'Let's try the bunkhouse,' Scott suggested, pointing to the low building. He liked to help out on the local ranches at round-up and had visited the Whangdoodle before. Buck scanned the area once again, then nudged the stallion into a walk.

They used the bunkhouse to give themselves cover from the ranch house. Both men watched the buildings warily, concentrating on the bunkhouse. Neither noticed the boy who stepped out on to the porch of the ranch house, stared at them, then retreated quietly inside again. At the back of the bunkhouse, Scott dismounted first and looked up at Buck, who slid quietly from his saddle beside him. Buck was about to ask what they should do next, when Scott looped his reins around a nail sticking out from a window shutter and walked round to the door. He pushed it open and went straight in. Buck hesitated for a moment and then followed, his heart pounding. The bunkhouse was deserted. Scott stood in the middle, glancing around at the clutter of belongings.

'We want blankets, canteens, coffee, mugs, knives, matches and guns,' he mused aloud.

'What if there'd been someone in here?' Buck hissed, acutely aware of trespassing.

'They'd have been too surprised to do anything,' Scott answered. 'We're supposed to be dead, remember?'

The only weapon in sight was a rifle hanging on the wall over a cot. Scott took it down and looked at the large side-hammer.

'This is a Spencer, right?' After a moment of fiddling, he withdrew the bullet tube from the stock. 'Not loaded.'

'See if there's any shells. It's better than nothing,' Buck answered. He was working busily, piling a few things on to the nearest bunk. He found a kit-bag under the low bunk and rapidly stuffed goods into it without bothering about more than a cursory glance at them. He rammed in a couple of shirts, a washkit, two boxes of matches and a coffee-stained mug. The smell from the mug reminded him of other essentials and he turned to the small stove in the centre of the room, where a coffee-pot stood.

Scott was loading the Spencer. He slid the refilled magazine tube home, studied the rifle a moment, then thumbed back the side hammer to test the mechanism. Just as he lifted the rifle, the bunkhouse door crashed open. Scott swung the rifle around and saw the woman there, holding a Winchester trained on him just as steadily as he held the Spencer on her. Scott recognized her at once: Mrs Clayton, John's mother.

SEVEN

'What are you doing here, you murderers?' demanded Mrs Clayton. The rancher's wife hadn't yet fixed her hair properly and still wore a large apron over her gingham dress, but she was fully awake and prepared to deal with her unwanted visitors.

'Murderers!' Scott exclaimed. 'Your husband and his men just tried to hang us. Look at the bruises on my neck.'

'It would be justice for what you did,' Mrs Clayton answered. The barrel of her rifle never waved from its alignment on Scott's chest.

'Your son drew his gun first,' Buck put in. 'He was the only one carrying a gun.'

'And he was aiming to kill Buck,' Scott said. His voice softened a little as he spoke again. 'I didn't mean to kill John and I'm sure sorry for causing you grief, ma'am. But that doesn't give your husband the right to break the law and string us both up for it.'

Mrs Clayton regarded him steadily. 'Are you going to shoot me too?' she asked.

Scott couldn't help admiring her courage but didn't lower his own gun. 'Not unless you force me to. We're not staying around where your husband can have another go at lynching us, and we don't have kit of our own. We'll take a few things and then ride out of here without anyone getting hurt. We don't have a lot to lose now, but you should think of your other kids.'

While Scott had been speaking, Buck started to gather a few more items. He lifted a jacket from one bunk and slipped it on, filling the pockets with odds and ends. He gave a brief cry of pleasure at finding a knife and took a few moments to fasten its sheath to his belt.

Mrs Clayton continued to watch Scott with bitter eyes. As the moments passed, her rifle began to waver as the effort of holding its weight to her shoulder began to tell. Scott noticed but made no comment on it.

'Maybe we should take a couple of spare mounts?' he suggested to Buck.

Buck paused in the act of shoving a pack of jerky into the kit bag. 'Steal horses? No way; I'm no damned horse-thief.' He spoke so vehemently that Scott didn't bother to press the point.

'Are you done?' Scott asked, still watching Mrs Clayton.

'*Vamos,*' Buck answered, swinging the kit bag over his shoulder.

The two young men faced Mrs Clayton. She had known both of them for years, and had seen them grow from boys to men just as her son, John, had grown. She had even attended the funeral of Buck's mother not long ago, and listened to the service conducted by Scott's father. Confronted by their familiar faces, she couldn't bring herself to pull the trigger. She slowly lowered the heavy rifle, her face drawn. Scott nodded slightly in appreciation, and lowered his own gun.

'Walk back to the house, ma'am. We'll be gone in a few minutes and your husband should be home soon.'

Mrs Clayton looked at them a moment longer. 'I'll trust God to punish those who need it.' She turned her back on them and walked away.

The dust of their departure had not long settled when Peter Clayton and his men arrived back at the ranch. Telling her younger children to remain indoors, Mrs Clayton went out to meet her husband. He rode to the front of the house and dismounted, tossing his horse's reins to the wrangler. The men swung away towards the corral to leave their weary, trail-dusty horses there.

'Those sons-of-bitches got away from us!' Peter Clayton exclaimed, striding up the porch steps. 'That black devil of Buck Heeley's damn near crushed Abe Johnson's chest.'

'They came here,' Mrs Clayton said quietly.

Her husband barely noticed the interruption, his energies concentrated on his own anger. 'I had ropes on both of them when that Bandit went plumb wild. You've never seen such a whirl-me-round and the pair of them got clean free and headed for the hills. Then Sheriff Millard showed up an' got real exercised about it all. Him worriting about Heeley and Beaumont when Abe's lying there with his ribs poking through his shirt.' Clayton paused for a moment, lifting his hat off his head to run his hand through his hair.

'They came here,' Mrs Clayton repeated more loudly. 'Freddie saw them ride up not an hour ago.'

'Here!' Clayton bellowed. 'Why that pair's got more nerve than a government mule! What in hell did they want here?'

'Goods. They daren't go back to town in case you come after them again. So they took things from the bunkhouse.'

Peter Clayton turned around in a small circle, bewildered and too outraged to think clearly. 'What goods?'

'Some clothes, cooking gear. Scott Beaumont had Oscar Crawford's old Spencer, that his pa used in the Civil War,' Mrs Clayton said.

'Crawford sure sets a store by that gun,' Peter Clayton said. For all his hatred of the two young men, it never occurred to him to ask if they had threatened his wife. 'Which way did they go?'

'They headed east,' Mrs Clayton answered. 'They may have been going towards Chinle Wash or the Chuskas.'

'That's Indian country. Buck's sure showing his skin there,' Peter Clayton added bitterly. 'It took the whole army to smoke the Navajo out of there in the first place. Finding just two men is nigh on impossible.'

'They killed our son,' Mrs Clayton said quietly.

Her husband looked at her. 'I set out this morning to see that they got what they deserved. I swore to punish them for murdering John.' He settled his hat firmly back on his head. 'Fix me some breakfast and I'll ride back to Navajo Rock when I've eaten. I want to send a telegram. This is a man-hunt, so I'm going to hire me the best hunter I can get.' He bent to kiss his wife briefly on the cheek and walked indoors.

Five days later Peter Clayton was waiting outside the cantina in Navajo Rock. There were usually some stools outside on the veranda and he took one, leaning back against the adobe wall. Some dark rain-clouds had been building steadily in the sky through the afternoon. He wanted rain; the ranch needed it for the grass and scrub to feed the cattle that the poor land barely supported. The rancher had developed a keen eye for weather during his years in Arizona and his instincts told him that the clouds weren't going to reach his range. Lightning flashed among the clouds, but if any rain fell, it would evaporate before it reached the dry earth below. Peter Clayton sighed.

At last, someone came riding into town from the north. Clayton leaned forward to study the new-comer as he approached. The stranger's horse was a good one, a light grey with black mane and tail and a white star showing on the pale grey of its face. Like any Westerner, Clayton had a good memory for horses and he knew he'd never seen the grey before. As they got closer, he looked at the rider. Other people were looking at the rider too. A newcomer was always an object of curiosity in a remote town like Navajo Rock, and this one was memorable. He was vividly handsome, with black hair, liquid, dark eyes and a full moustache. When he passed a dark-haired woman on the street, he lifted his broad-brimmed black hat and smiled brilliantly at her, acknowledging her interest as perfectly natural. She stared hard for a moment before hurrying on. The rider's clothes matched the quality of his horse. He wore black trousers, boots and frock-coat, but he had a red silk cravat, a red-and-gold brocade waistcoat and silver spurs. The eye-catching finery tended to make people overlook the two 3 Model Smith & Wessons in the cross-draw holsters.

Peter Clayton stood up, catching the newcomer's eye. The stranger rode towards him and halted the grey with a light touch on the reins.

'Jonah Durrell?' Clayton asked.

The stranger smiled. 'I sure am. Mr Clayton, I presume?' He had the clipped accent of a New Englander. When Peter Clayton nodded, Durrell dismounted gracefully. 'I'd like to settle Chinook before we talk.'

'Livery barn's down there.' Clayton pointed the way. Though he was on the veranda and Durrell was on the street, he could tell that the handsome man was taller than himself, and probably broader across the shoulders. 'Beer?'

'Very welcome,' Durrell answered, turning his horse towards the barn.

He joined Peter Clayton inside the cantina a few minutes later. The rancher had wired Durrell on the morning of Buck's and Scott's escape. Durrell had been on the trail ever since but it barely showed. As he sat down, Jonah Durrell brushed a touch of trail-dust from his immaculate coat and removed his hat to show glossy hair. He hung the hat up carefully, flipping back his hair from his face. Chavez's wife brought the beer and Durrell smiled at her, provoking a rare smile in return. Clayton was unimpressed by the hunter's easy charm.

'I didn't bring you here to flirt,' he snapped.

Durrell repressed a smile at the rancher's tone.

'I want you to find me two men. The men who killed my eldest son,' Clayton said.

'What should I do with them when I've found them?' Durrell asked, his tone businesslike. 'Has the local law put out a reward for them?'

'Fifty dollars each. I just want them dead. They confessed to killing John all right; even Buck's father'll admit that. I want to see their bodies.'

'If they've been on the run since you wired me, they could be a long way off now.'

Peter Clayton shook his head. 'Not them. Buck Heeley's never lived anyplace else. He's part Navajo and they chose to come back to this desert. Buck couldn't stand to leave Dinetah.'

Jonah Durrell sipped his beer as he considered the job. He usually worked around the Colorado mining-fields and he didn't know this red-brown country of canyons and mesas. On the other hand, this new country would be interesting and his name would get known wider afield. For all his affectations of vanity, Jonah Durrell was an intelligent man. Working as a bounty hunter kept him challenged and fit, and paid well enough for him to indulge his taste for fine living. 'Describe them. Tell me everything about Buck Heeley and Scott Beaumont.'

The rancher did as asked, starting with a vivid description of Scott's orange corkscrew hair. Durrell smiled and smoothed down his own black hair. He listened for nearly five minutes, sipping his beer now and again, while the rancher spoke. Peter Clayton had known both the young men for years and half-remembered anecdotes were mixed in with the descriptions, along with comparisons to his dead son. Durrell realized that Clayton knew the young men far better than he had supposed.

'Will they stick together?' he asked.

'Oh, sure.' Clayton answered without even thinking. 'Buck and Scott have been pals since they were both knee-high to a grasshopper. They always stuck together against anyone else.' There was a touch of resentment in his tone; his son had never found such a good friend.

'I'll take the job,' Durrell decided. 'Five hundred dollars each, dead or alive.'

Peter Clayton held out his hand and the two men shook on the deal.

'I'll rest up overnight, give Chinook a breather,' Durrell decided. 'Is there anywhere besides here I can get a room?' He found the cantina's mixed smells of tequila and chilli distasteful.

'Stop at my place,' Clayton offered. 'It's only another hour's ride and I can loan you one of the remuda hosses for a remount.'

'Thank you,' Durrell said graciously.

As the two men headed for the door, Clayton

spoke again. 'Oh, one more thing. Buck Heeley rides a black stallion. I want that hoss if you can get it but it's a mean critter.'

Durrell nodded, keeping his feelings on that to himself.

As they left the cantina, they ran straight into Tom Heeley and the dark-haired woman who had been looking at Durrell earlier.

'Who's this?' Heeley asked Clayton abruptly.

Peter Clayton made the introductions, telling Durrell that the woman was Lizzie Hillerman, Buck's oldest, married sister. Heeley glanced at the cross-draw holsters that Durrell wore.

'Expecting trouble?' he asked, his eyes cold with suspicion.

Durrell smiled brightly. 'This is pretty rough country.'

'If you stay round here, you could run into trouble,' Lizzie interrupted, dislike clear on her face. Her expression didn't change as she turned to the rancher. 'You've got no right to bring a bounty hunter in to look for Buck and Scott.'

'They murdered my son,' Clayton snapped.

'Your precious John insulted our mother,' Mary returned with spirit. 'You reckon you're better'n us because we're part Navajo, but at least Navajo don't say one thing and do another. You go to church but you sure don't act Christian!'

Jonah Durrell repressed a smile at her sharp remark and stood quietly, taking his chance to hear the other side of the story.

'And when was murder a Christian act?' Peter

Clayton answered heatedly.

'I still say you got no right to bring in a hunter,' Heeley interrupted. 'If he hurts my son, you and your ranch don't get so much as a single biscuit from my store.'

'I can get all my goods at the Hubbell trading store,' Clayton answered.

Heeley spotted the sheriff crossing the street towards them. 'Millard! Tell Clayton to send this damned bounty hunter back where he come from.'

Sheriff Millard climbed on to the veranda outside the cantina. A few other people had heard the voices and were hanging around outside nearby buildings, listening. The sheriff stared coolly at Durrell, who nodded politely, the most relaxed person present.

'What's your name?' the sheriff asked.

'Jonah Durrell. I usually work up Colorado way.'

Millard nodded. 'I've heard of you.'

'Tell him he can't work around here,' Heeley insisted.

'Can't do that, Tom,' Millard said, pushing his white Stetson to the back of his head. 'Buck and Scott skipped jail, and I know they had a mighty good reason,' he added, holding up a hand to forestall arguments. 'But there's money for them. If Clayton and Durrell want to make an arrangement between them privately, there's nothing I can do agin it.'

Tom Heeley glanced once at Durrell, then dismissed him and turned to Peter Clayton.

'Don't do this,' he said. 'You pay a hunter to kill my son and you'll never be able to show your face in this town again.'

Peter Clayton flushed with anger. 'You don't own this town, Heeley. That no-account store of yours might be the oldest thing here but this is a town now, not just a few adobes around your trading post. The Mex might do like you say, but the white folks here are free and independent.'

Tom Heeley started to answer then stopped. A look of tired resignation took over from the anger. 'If you don't understand now, you never will.'

'All I understand is that your boy, or his damned friend, killed my son. I want justice for that,' Clayton hissed.

'No, Mr Clayton,' Mary Hillerman said clearly. 'You want revenge.' With that, she took her father's arm and led him away back towards the store.

Millard nodded. 'Heeley's got a point. You bring in some paid outsider, there's plenty of folks in town won't cotton none to that.'

'I aim to see my John gets justice, even if you won't, Sheriff,' Peter Clayton retorted. 'Buck killed my son and no one in this one-horse town gives a damn. You all stick up for Buck like he was the President himself. Well I aim to bring him down no matter what. You can't stop me.' On those words he turned away to fetch his horse and leave the town behind him.

EIGHT

As predicted, Scott and Buck had retreated to the vast Canyon de Chelly complex for a few days. Scott suggested camping in one of the ancient stone ruins of little square houses built high into alcoves along the towering cliffs. Buck vetoed the idea, pointing out that they couldn't get the horses up the cliffs and that they needed to stay close to their mounts. His other reasons were less tangible, rooted in Navajo fears of death and ghosts passed on to him by his family. Instead, they stayed in the green strip of trees and shrubs that bordered the shallow, wandering Tsaile Creek. They didn't speak much about what had happened, but explored the canyon complex together. The towering red-orange cliffs, streaked with black, rose above them and shut out the rest of the world. Cut off, they almost lost track of time.

Eventually, their aimless wanderings brought them to Canyon del Muerto.

'Oh, death, where is thy sting?' Scott quoted, gazing around.

The Navajo orchards were here until the army cut

them down, Buck told him. 'Five thousand peach trees and the army destroyed the lot.'

'I guess some general didn't like peaches,' Scott answered.

Buck gave him a half-hearted glare. He barely remembered those times, but his extended Navajo family had been starved, frozen and rounded up by the army as they sought to control the tribe some twenty years earlier. His mother's Navajo relatives were the only family he knew, so Scott's frivolity annoyed him. Buck slid from his saddle and loosened Bandit's cinch. The stallion lowered his head straightaway and began to graze. Scott followed his friend's example and sat beside him in the twilight shade under the cliffs.

'I wish there was someplace we could get some corn for them,' he said, looking at the two horses.

'Or something for us. I don't mind if I don't eat another kangaroo rat in my life,' Buck said. The few items he had got from the Whangdoodle's bunkhouse had been eaten already.

'We wouldn't even have kangaroo rats if your uncle hadn't taught you to set traps,' Scott acknowledged. He pulled up a stalk of tough grass and chewed on it.

'More useful than knowing the dates of the presidents,' Buck teased. They lapsed into silence for a while. Having thought of the school, Buck was wondering what was happening at the little store building in Navajo Rock. It would seem very quiet with only Pa and Mae there now. Almost before he knew it, Buck was longing for home so hard it hurt.

'Pa would give us some coffee and stores and stuff,' Buck said suddenly.

'I'm not going back to Navajo Rock,' Scott insisted. The bruises on his neck were fading now to yellow and green.

'Not to surrender,' Buck replied, sitting upright and speaking urgently. 'I could sneak in after dark. We could just get a proper supply of kit, and more guns. Pa won't turn me in, you know that.'

Scott did know it. He also knew that the odds and ends of equipment they had weren't enough to camp out for any length of time or for travelling elsewhere. Reluctantly, he nodded. 'All right. We'll head back to town.'

The sun was setting when Buck rode slowly towards Navajo Rock. His heart rose at the sight of the familiar landscape as he approached cautiously from the west. He halted behind a rock outcropping a few hundred yards from town and tethered Bandit to some rabbit-brush.

'I know we're close to home, but stay there,' he said softly, patting the stallion's neck. The horse whickered softly and settled down to doze.

Buck kept to the shadows as he moved between the handful of adobes behind the store building. He froze as someone came out to use a privy, only moving on when the man was peacefully settled inside his wooden outbuilding. He reached the store's yard without being seen and slunk around the side of the stable. Glancing about, Buck set off over the open space of the yard. He was half-way across when his high-strung senses heard someone coming down the side alley. Which way to run? After a moment's panic, he dived back to the stable and crouched in the shadow there. He knew from games of hide-and-seek with his sisters that their dark colouring was hard to see in the poor light. Buck thought he recognized the newcomer's shape; his guess was confirmed when the man moved into the faint light coming through the curtained window. It was George Beaumont, Scott's father. The preacher knocked loudly on the back door and was admitted by Tom Heeley. Buck's heart sank as he watched. He had little hope of getting help from Scott's father.

Perhaps he was only on a brief visit; Scott's father had never visited much before. Buck crept across the yard, his heart pounding, and crouched under the open window. Fortunately, the curtains had been drawn and Buck could listen without much chance of being seen.

'Well, I ain't sorry about it,' his father was saying. 'Peter Clayton was aiming to string them up there and then.'

'They killed a man,' the preacher answered. 'They broke the most important law of God and they must accept the punishment.'

Heeley kept his voice reasonable but Buck could hear the effort it took. 'They did accept it; they done came back and gave themselves up, didn't they? I'm plumb proud of them for that. But Clayton was acting outside the law too. Lynching a man without trial is murder too, dammit!'

'We must keep law here. Without strong law this

place will be as infested with sin as Lincoln County in New Mexico,' the preacher lectured.

'Does your idea of law include lynch mobs and bounty hunters?' Heeley asked.

The preacher's voice thundered as if he were delivering a sermon in church. 'Joy shall be in Heaven over one sinner that repenteth, more than over ninety-and-nine just persons, which need no repentance. Those are the words of Saint Luke and our children must listen to them.'

Crouching below the window, Buck grinned to himself. He wondered what the preacher would do if he knew that one of the children concerned was listening to him at that moment.

'Who says they haven't repented of killing John Clayton?' Heeley demanded. 'That's a bounty killer that Clayton's hired to find them. He's set a killer after your son and mine.'

The grin vanished from Buck's face.

'An eye for an eye and a life for a life,' the preacher answered solemnly.

'I'm talking about our sons! Quit preaching at me!' Heeley answered. There was an ominous moment of silence.

'O, miserable sinner,' said the preacher. 'Your child has led mine into the paths of sin and hellfire. I shall never rest until I have seen them returned to the ways of God. I shall pray for you and beg the Lord to forgive your wicked arrogance and pride. Pride was the sin of Lucifer, for which he fell from God's grace. Your family shall fall too.'

'Leave my house now.' Although Tom Heeley

spoke quietly, it was the kind of voice that Buck never argued with.

The preacher must have recognized the tone too, for Buck could hear him walking across the wooden floor.

'If I see your son or mine, I shall turn them over to the proper law to be dealt with according to Justice,' Preacher George said.

Buck had to run across the yard to the safe shadows around the stable, so he never heard what his father said. He watched silently as the preacher left. Yellow lamplight flickered into the yard as the door opened and closed. Buck longed to go to its warm welcome, but his nerve failed him. There was a bitterness in his heart as he slipped away into the dusk.

He returned to Scott without any of the things they wanted.

'Your father was there,' he said, stripping the stallion's heavy saddle off. 'I didn't dare go in.'

Scott grunted a reply as he stirred the tiny campfire. Brilliant sparks flew up from the fast-burning greasewood. He didn't blame Buck for avoiding the preacher but he didn't feel any better about their situation.

Buck watched for a moment as Bandit lay down in the clumsy way that horses have, and began to roll. The absurdity of the stallion kicking his legs in the air and grunting as he squirmed about always made Buck smile, even now. Leaving the horse to enjoy himself, Buck returned to the fire and took the mug of coffee Scott offered.

'Pa also mentioned something about a bounty

hunter,' Buck said, sniffing at the coffee. Scott had never been much good at making coffee.

'A bounty hunter?' Scott repeated.

'He said Peter Clayton's hired someone; that's all I know.' Buck took a sip of the coffee. He didn't mention that Scott's father wanted to turn them in again.

Scott stared into the leaping flames of the fire, his face tingling with the warmth. 'I'm not going back to be hanged.'

'No bounty man can find us in Canyon de Chelly,' Buck answered. 'Clayton can't keep paying him forever. We'll hide out, maybe till the snow comes if we have to.'

'What about food?' Scott asked.

Buck grinned suddenly. 'Plenty of beef on the Whangdoodle.'

'So there is.'

They moved on at first light the next morning. Neither horse was a trained cow-pony but Scott's experience on round ups was good enough for him to be able to rope a cow from his pinto. They chivvied the bellowing longhorn away from the open range to the mouth of a wash and slaughtered her there.

'How the hell did those buffalo-skinners manage?' Scott grumbled as he attempted to cut away the skin with the only good knife they had.

'Proper equipment,' Buck answered, tugging at a flap of hide.

The horses were left a short distance away to graze while the men butchered the tough cow. Longhorns were notoriously uncooperative in life and this one was just as stubborn in death. Scott sawed at the thick hide while Buck held it taut. Both of them had blood and scraps of flesh all over their hands.

'It looks like a scene from Macbeth,' Scott commented. 'Will all great Neptune's ocean wash this blood clean from my hand?'

'Shut up and cut some meat,' Buck answered tolerantly.

They worked in silence for a few minutes, hacking chunks of meat from the carcass. It was a messy job and their already grubby clothes got worse. Buck was wiping futilely at a blood patch on his pants when he heard Bandit snorting fiercely. He looked up and saw the stallion standing alertly to attention, its eyes and ears fixed on a distant point beyond the safety of the wash. Scott looked up too.

'He's probably scented a mare,' he remarked.

'We can't have him go chasing off now,' answered Buck uneasily. He hurried to catch up with the stallion and loop his reins around a juniper bush. With some control established, he moved cautiously forward to see the open range. The nearest dot of movement was a man on a grey horse, leading a bay mount, and heading straight for the wash. Buck moved slowly out of sight then dashed back to Scott.

'Someone's coming directly. Stop cutting and start packing.' He began piling meat on to flaps of the hide.

'They can't know we're here,' Scott answered, doing the same anyway.

'Well he sure seems to.' Instinct made Buck glance

upwards. Sure enough, two turkey vultures were circling high above, waiting for them to leave the carcass so they could pick over the remains. The rider had spotted the waiting birds and was coming to investigate.

Buck and Scott hurriedly thrust chunks of raw meat into their packs. Their horses snorted at the smell. Bandit sidled around and then stopped, throwing his head up to listen. Buck sprang aboard even as he heard the chink of a hoof against rock somewhere near the mouth of the wash. As he gathered up the reins, Bandit let out a tremendous challenging whinny, shaking himself with the effort.

'Knob-headed fool,' Buck cursed under his breath. He swung the stallion around and pressed him into a gallop. From behind came the sound of fast-moving horses.

Jonah Durrell had heard Bandit's challenge and knew it for the call of a stallion scenting a stranger. He charged, hoping to catch the unseen men on foot, and slipped his rifle from its boot on his saddle. Jonah was proud of his rifle. It was the latest model from Winchester, the 1886, with an octagonal barrel and checkered engraving on the black walnut stock. It was an elegantly finished weapon and still practical. Jonah Durrell liked to possess beautiful things, but never made the mistake of sacrificing utility for show, especially in weapons and horses. His grey, Chinook, raced eagerly across the dry ground and into the mouth of the wash. At the end of its rope trailed a bay on a loan from the Whangdoodle. Durrell had heard horses moving rapidly even before they came into view. A quick look at the black and the pinto was enough to tell him he had found his men. Pulling up, he threw the rifle to his shoulder and took a quick shot before they vanished around a curve of the wash. Durrell saw dirt spray from the side of the wash near the black. The rider ducked away slightly but never hesitated. Durrell pushed the rifle away and switched horses without bothering to dismount in-between. The bay was fresher and he urged it in pursuit, trusting his grey, Chinook, to follow without guidance.

The soft ground showed the tracks of the galloping horses clearly enough for him to read them without slowing. Durrell drew one of his Smith & Wessons and held it ready in case he ran into an ambush. It wasn't likely; these weren't hardened criminals and they could have ambushed him to begin with instead of running. All the same, he was ready for trouble, his dark eyes glowing brightly with cool pleasure as he chased the two fugitives deeper into the maze of washes and arroyos. He was pleased with the way the bay ran. The horse belonged to the Whangdoodle and he was using it to ride relay so he would always have a fresh horse. Both mounts were in good condition and grain-fed. Durrell had been told about Bandit's speed but the fugitives' horses had been living rough for nearly two weeks now. His horses would outlast the two he was chasing now.

Durrell sat lightly in the saddle as the bay galloped steadily through the twists and turns of the arroyos. The one he was following forked in two but he could read the signs in the churned ground and broken branches of a juniper without needing to slow down. Durrell took the left fork and kept going, his gaze flickering between the ground and the landscape ahead. The creek ran wide and shallow in this arroyo, flowing smoothly around sandbars and rock. The walls of the arroyo curved around an outcrop of pink and buff rock, now rising some twenty feet above Durrell's head. The tracks he was following ran into the creek but there were no marks or splashes on the far side.

Durrell smiled to himself as he rode into the creek. Bright water splashed up around the bay's legs and belly as it galloped steadily on. Durrell kept watch on both sides of the creek, waiting to see where the tracks would re-emerge. He caught a glimpse of piled rocks further ahead where one wall of the arroyo had once crumbled into slabs. Difficult to get a horse through, but not impossible for a good rider. No doubt they hoped to lose him on the rocks but Durrell was confident of finding some sign. Horseshoes could leave marks on rocks, especially where the going was difficult.

With his eyes on the land and his thoughts on tracking, Jonah Durrell failed to see the slight eddy in the creek. The bay galloped straight into the hidden hole in the creek bed and fell, dumping its rider face first into the cold water. Durrell was taken completely by surprise when the horse fell, but instinctively kicked himself clear of the saddle. He hit the water sideways and went right under, getting a noseful of water. He kicked around wildly for a moment until his feet hit bottom and he struggled upright. Even as he snorted water from his nose and shook his head, the flailing horse soused him again, Durrell cursed loudly and solidly, as he wiped water from his eyes with one hand and drew another gun with his right. No shots came his way. After a quick look around, Durrell waded out of the water and examined his guns. The brief soaking hadn't damaged them but they should be properly cleaned soon. After making that essential check, he turned his attention to the horses. Chinook had left the creek of his own accord and was peacefully cropping grass on the far bank. The bay was still standing in the water, shivering.

'Come on, you fool, ewe-necked critter,' Durrell said, wading back into the knee-deep water to take the reins. The bay was reluctant to move at first and when he coaxed it to the bank alongside the grey, the bay was lame on its off fore. Durrell examined it gently, running his hands down the bay's leg. It wasn't broken, luckily, but the bay had sprained something when it put its leg into the hole and fell. Durrell straightened up, patting the miserable horse on the neck.

'Nothing for you now but some good rest,' he told it, pulling the horse's ears through his hands to warm it after the shock and ducking. 'It's a good five hours from here to the ranch but we'll take it steady.'

Only after seeing to the horse did Durrell think of himself. He was even wetter than the bay, his hair plastered to his head and his sleeves dripping water. Durrell prised off his boots and removed his frock-coat, spreading it to dry in the hot sun.

'There's some men would pay plenty good money to see me mussed up like this,' he told the horses wryly, fully aware of how comical the fall must have looked. 'And a few women who'd pay to see this,' he added, stripping off shirt and trousers. He admired his broad chest for a moment, then grinned at himself and went to fetch a towel from the grey's saddle-bags.

NINE

Buck backed down from the rocks, giving a thumbs up signal to Scott waiting with the horses in the wash below. He climbed back down, moving quietly, and joined his friend. 'He went belly-first into that hole like a dog in a pond,' Buck reported.

Scott grinned. 'Wish I'd seen that. Smart thinking to lead him into it.'

'It sure was,' Buck agreed immodestly. 'He's done lamed one of his horses and given up chasing us.'

'Great. Let's push on a bit then stop somewhere's and fry us up some steak,' Scott said avidly.

They circled east and north towards the outlets of Canyon de Chelley again. After a couple of hours, they found a pleasant spot by a tiny creek and made camp there. The horses tore at thin, yellowy grass while Scott cooked chunks of beef over a small fire. The rich smell of the meat filled the air, overwhelming the usual scents of dust and wilting leaves common to the high desert.

'Oh, God, that smells good,' Buck remarked, his stomach rumbling.

'Not a bad day's work,' Scott said, using the point of a knife to move the meat in the bottom of the pan. 'Got us some food and saw off a bounty hunter.'

Buck laughed. 'I don't reckon we'll have much trouble with him. He was all dressed up like a pup with a new collar but them fine duds won't look the same after getting soused in the creek. I bet he'll go back to the city by the end of the week.'

'He might have more stick-to-it than that,' Scott answered. 'He can't have any reputation as a hunter if he quits that quick.'

'True. But I never saw him afore. I bet fifty dollars we can keep away from him in this country. It was smart of him to take a look-see at what the vultures were circling, but he won't get that lucky again,' Buck insisted cheerfully.

Scott grinned, leaning over the pan to get a good lungful of the scent. 'This smells better than any cigar.'

Buck nodded. 'We'll keep on moving. The bounty hunter'll figure out he can't catch us out here and he'll quit. Give it two, three weeks and I'll go home on the quiet. I'll speak to Pa and get some goods for us. He can tell us iffen it's safe for us to go home. We've just got to wait out Clayton.'

'He can't stay that mad at us for ever,' Scott agreed, mellowed by the smell of the cooking beef. 'He won't dare try stringing us up again.'

Buck nodded. 'Is that done yet?'

Scott speared a chunk of beef on the point of his knife and examined it. 'Close enough. Let's eat.'

There was no argument on that.

*

In spite of his ducking, Jonah Durrell still had his usual air of elegance when he returned to the Whangdoodle that evening.

'At least I've now seen them both,' he remarked to Mrs Clayton as she took his crumpled shirt to iron it. His clothing had dried quickly enough in the hot sun but coat and trousers were both coated in dust and the long riding boots had lost their polish. However, neither his disarray not his fast-growing dark stubble could detract from his good looks and self confidence.

'Betsy, take his coat and beat the dirt from it,' Mrs Clayton instructed her eldest daughter.

Jonah smiled as he handed the coat to the fifteen-year-old girl, noticing her pretty blonde hair and blossoming figure. She noticed his look and stared back with open interest for a moment before blushing and hurrying away. His dark eyes sparkled with silent amusement as he sat down at the scrubbed wooden table in the ranch house.

The parlour/dining-room was a pleasant place, that appealed to his sense of order and homeliness. There was a varnished whatnot in the corner displaying ornaments and a steadily ticking china clock. A pair of home-made braided rugs were set in front of the two upholstered armchairs by the fire and there was a pretty sampler on one wall. Mrs Clayton fussed around the guest, seeing to his clothes and comfort even while she complained of his failure and return.

'Now they know someone's after them,' she said. 'Take your boots off and Simon will polish them when he's fetched more kindling.'

'No need, thank you,' Durrell answered. 'I'll take care of them myself.' He leaned back in the wooden chair. 'If they're butchering steers, they're running short of food. What other stores are there out here?'

Mrs Clayton snorted. 'There's Hubbell's trading post, fifty miles to the south. We've told them to watch out for Buck and Scott and posted a reward there.'

'Good work.'

'This isn't work,' Mrs Clayton retorted. She stood still for a moment, resting a hand on her hip as she gazed down at the seated man. 'They killed my son. I want them punished for it.'

Durrell raised an eyebrow at her matter-of-fact tone. 'They came back to town to accept a punishment.'

'And now they've run again.' She tucked a loose strand of hair behind her ear. 'They killed John. I want them punished.'

'I'll do my best to see you get what you desire,' Durrell promised with an air of gallantry. 'If you wish to see the pair of them dead, then I shall kill them for you.'

Mrs Clayton studied him for a minute, as if searching for mockery. 'That's what you're paid for.'

He simply nodded. There was no point in arguing with someone set on vengeance and, besides, there was a decent sum of money involved. Durrell sat quietly at the table while supper was prepared. He thought about the two young men who had gotten themselves into trouble, and tried to guess what they would do next. Mrs Clayton had described Scott and Buck as criminals but Durrell could see that they had restricted their thefts to the Whangdoodle. He guessed that when they needed more food, they would come back to the ranch.

Peter Clayton came bustling in for supper with his family. He glowered at the hunter, clearly feeling that Durrell should have been back on the range with a fresh horse. Durrell preferred to get an extra night of home comforts and took no notice.

'You should get out and search for tracks afore they get blown all to hell,' Clayton told Durrell as he reached for the coffee-pot.

'They'll be miles away,' Durrell answered unworriedly. 'They've got too much sense to stay where they were last seen.'

'What are you going to do?'

Jonah Durrell helped himself to potatoes. 'Spare me one of your hands to ride around with for a few days. Someone who knows the whole range well. They'll be back here, and I want to be ready for them.'

Peter Clayton glared at the confident younger man. 'Back here?'

'Sure.' Durrell passed the dish of potatoes to Betsy, his dark eyes flirting briefly with her. 'Probably not to the ranch house, but back on your range, sure as eggs are eggs.' He looked at the rancher calmly.

Peter Clayton sensed something of the other man's quick intelligence, and accepted his word. 'All

right, you can take Billy Hargreaves and Oscar
Crawford with you.'

'I'll find some place where I can get the drop on
Heeley and Beaumont,' Durrell said. 'I could chase
them round this open country for ever. Better to
figure out where they're likely to go, and wait for
them.' As he spoke, he was aware of Betsy stealing
glances at him. He made no response, and had no
intention of so much as kissing the rancher's daughter, but her attention pleased his vanity. There were
some compensations for this particular job, after all.

When he rode out the next morning, Jonah Durrell
looked as smart as he had when he arrived in town.
Oscar Crawford stared rudely at him before speaking.

'Which way?' he asked, his eyes full of contempt
and jealousy. Crawford was a short and knotty gnome
of a man, cursed with red hair and skin that peeled
endlessly under the desert sun. He disliked the handsome bounty hunter on sight.

Durrell wasn't in the least bit disturbed. 'You're
the guides, but I reckon we should start over that way.
If they've gone back to Canyon de Chelly, they'll have
to approach from the east, right?'

'Of course,' Billy Hargreaves said contemptuously,
even though he hadn't thought about it. He turned
his horse and eased it into a jog. As they rode, he
continued to stare at Durrell. 'Why don't you use
Colts?' he asked.

'Because the Smith and Wesson has almost perfect
balance and it's quicker to reload,' Durrell answered.

Billy Hargreaves sniffed. 'I like a solid-framed gun,' he insisted, patting his Colt.

'I never had one of these blow up in my face yet,' Jonah Durrell told him. The time passed quickly as they rode, arguing the merits of different guns.

The range to the east had saltbrush flats broken with canyons; arroyos and sudden outcrops of rock. A brilliant blue sky arched above the red and grey land, which was decorated with clumps of grass, rabbitbush, creosote bush and spiny shrubs. Every change of view seemed to show more of the same. A few tough cattle grazed here and there but there were no signs of human life once the ranch buildings were lost to sight. To Jonah Durrell, it looked desolate and poor.

'Must get damned bleak up here in winter,' he remarked eventually. 'If you get anything like a winter,' he added, squinting briefly at the blazing sun.

'We get winters all right,' Crawford told him, rubbing a few flakes of sunburned skin from his nose as he spoke. 'Snow and blizzards an' all.' He reined in his horse to look over the valley below. 'This's about the edge of our range. That land kind of belongs to the Navajo.' He pointed to a round building made of stone slabs with a domed roof. It was perched on a ridge with a long view down the slope of the valley.

'That's Old Woman Endocheeney's place,' Billy Hargreaves said. 'She's always complaining about our beef messing up her spring.'

Durrell could see the little flock of goats down in

the valley, being watched by a boy in his early teens.
'Where's the next nearest water to this spring?'

Oscar Crawford knew the answer straight away.
'There's a seep ten miles back that way, runs to
Keams Canyon eventually. That'll be dry now. Next
closest is Chinle Wash coming out of Canyon de
Chelly.' He pointed slightly north of east, to the end
of Defiance Plateau that reared itself in the distance,
with the Chuskas beyond.

That meant Old Woman Endocheeney's spring
was the only water available to the fugitives after leaving their hideout in the canyon. They would almost
certainly come this way to water their horses.

Durrell took a long look, then set Chinook carefully down the slope ahead. The ground here was
scattered with loose shale, with clumps of yellow flow-
ers growing here and there amongst the broken
rock.

'Was there a quarry here?' Durrell asked. He
couldn't imagine what anyone would have mined out
here, but he didn't know how else the rock might
have got broken up.

'Nope. It's just like this,' Crawford answered, leaning back as his horse slithered over some loose rocks.

They spent the next day and a half scouting the
whole area thoroughly. Durrell insisted that they stay
away from the Navajos and their flocks, not wanting
to cause trouble. He explored the draws and canyons
to the east of the valley, asking detailed questions
about the trails. There were very few formal trails in
this almost uninhabited country, and he guessed that
the fugitives would have the sense to avoid the most

obvious ones. On the other hand, the broken country limited the choices available to anyone travelling into the wide valley from the Canyon de Chelly. Jonah Durrell's success as a bounty hunter was based not just on his courage and gun-skill, but on his ability to out-think the men he was pursuing. After watching him at work, and being quizzed in detail, the Whangdoodle men found themselves reluctantly admiring the dandy bounty hunter, who still somehow looked as stylish as he had when leaving the ranch house.

'Why don't you take up law work?' Crawford asked as they paused to water the horses at the spring.

'Have you any idea what lawmen do when they're not arresting owlhoots?' Jonah answered, dismounting to stretch his legs. He bent a couple of times to ease the kinks from his body and straightened the sleeves of his coat.

Oscar Crawford shook his head.

'They collect taxes; they find lost children, and they write reports and log books. It's very dull and it doesn't pay very well. And you're a target for every smart-mouth wandering into town who wants to show his friends what kind of a real man he is. I'll stick to chasing fugitives around this desolate bit of no-good land.'

'Have you figured out yet where to find them?' Crawford asked.

Durrell nodded. 'I've got the most likely spots picked out.'

'So what do we do?' Hargreaves asked.

'You better go back to the ranch,' Durrell told

Crawford. 'Come back in a couple days with some grub. Billy, I want you to be my back-up.'

Hargreaves' face lit up. 'Just give me a chance of shooting down that no account half-breed and his pal. I hate the way Beaumont shows off his book-learning all the while.'

'What iffen they don't come through the spot you picked?' Crawford asked.

Durrell grinned. 'I've got a spot picked where I can watch the trail and keep an eye on the valley and this spring. If Buck Heeley's the kind of horseman you all make out, he'll stop here to water his mount before going on to Whangdoodle land where he might be seen and have to run. If they come past me another way, I'll see them here and be on the trail behind them. If they're heading to the ranch, they won't be watching their back trail. I can get them that way.'

'Oh.' Crawford hadn't thought the situation through and was impressed by Durrell's forward planning.

Durrell recognized the look of wonder and admiration on the cowhand's sunburned face. It never ceased to surprise him that what seemed so obvious to him tended to elude other men. With only a little luck, the fugitives would be as slow in tactical thinking as most others were.

'You got a real smart headpiece on you,' Crawford admitted. 'How long you reckon you'll be waiting?'

That was harder to estimate but Durrell spoke as confidently as before. 'Probably another couple of days. I should be back at the Whangdoodle inside of a week.'

Crawford nodded. 'I'll tell them that. We need some good news.'

Durrell suppressed the thought that it wouldn't be good news for the Heeleys or the Beaumonts. It wasn't his job to point out inconsistencies in the customer's arguments. He raised his hand in a farewell gesture as Crawford turned his horses away.

'See you in a week,' Crawford called.

In the event, Jonah Durrell only had to wait a day and a half before Buck Heeley rode into his gunsights. He came alert as he heard the muffled thud from somewhere up on the trail. He listened, almost holding his breath, and caught the fainter sounds of a horse moving steadily. Long experience told him that the noise he had heard was the sound of a hoof against rock. His own horses were tethered in a shallow rocky hollow a few hundred yards away from where he waited. Billy Hargreaves was there too. The cowhand hadn't liked the idea of being kept in the background but Durrell had insisted. His main reason for keeping Hargreaves away from the ambush was that he didn't trust the cowhand to act sensibly in a crisis. Durrell also liked the idea of riding back to the Whangdoodle and announcing that he had caught the two fugitives single-handed.

The bounty hunter had chosen his spot in a shady cleft between the rock walls of this cut through the edge of the valley. The horse he could hear was approaching from his right, still hidden by a bend in the canyon and a pair of gnarled Russian olive trees. The thin goat trail along this canyon was quite passable but it wasn't the easiest route from Canyon de Chelly to the valley. Whoever was riding along would be concentrating on his horse, helping it pick its way around all the loose rock.

Durrell could only hear one horse moving, but his worry was relieved when the rider came into view, barely twenty feet away. It was Buck Heeley all right, mounted on the splendid black horse that Durrell had glimpsed before. He felt a momentary sympathy for the fugitive; Heeley was unshaven and wore a filthy shirt, with bloodstained sleeves and a tear on the shoulder. The stallion too was showing signs of the hunt. His coat lacked its usual gloss and he had a round grass belly rather than the leaner line of a grain-fed horse. More important to Jonah Durrell, the only weapon that Heeley carried was a knife.

The bounty hunter waited a few moments, watching his target approach at a leisurely pace and listening for another horse. When he was sure Buck was on his own, Durrell lifted his Smith & Wesson and moved into view, cocking the gun as he held it steadily on the young man.

'Take it easy,' he warned, as Buck reined in the stallion.

TEN

There was a flicker of surprise on Heeley's dark face, rapidly schooled into Indian indifference. 'You're the bounty hunter Clayton's hired.'

'I am,' Durrell answered, standing a few feet in front of the horse and slightly to one side.

'We done killed John Clayton but it was self-defence.' Heeley spoke evenly, stating a fact.

'I'm not paid to care,' Durrell answered. 'I'm paid to fetch you back to Clayton, on your saddle or strapped across it.' He was aware that surely Scott Beaumont had to be nearby, and Beaumont had a rifle. Durrell couldn't afford to get caught in conversation while a second enemy could be approaching. 'Dismount,' he ordered.

Heeley kicked his feet free of his wooden stirrups and did as he was told. 'Take us home; to Navajo Rock,' he asked. 'If you take us to the Whangdoodle, Peter Clayton will string us up there and then. Hand us to Sheriff Millard; let the law handle this.'

'It's not my look-out if Clayton gives you a rope necktie and then gets himself arrested for murder,'

121

Durrell remarked cheerfully. 'Take that knife out slowly and toss it over there.'

Again, Heeley did as he was told. The knife clattered against rock and bounced out of sight under a tamarisk. Jonah Durrell held his gun steady on Heeley while he fished a length of rawhide thong from his coat pocket with his other hand.

'Turn around.'

Heeley turned, bringing his hands together behind his back.

Durrell walked to him, watching his prisoner intently. 'I don't have to kill you outright to bring you in,' he warned. 'I can just shoot you in the back of the knee.' He was too busy watching the man to take much notice of the horse.

Durrell was aware of the stallion's presence, but didn't notice the horse's ears going back when he approached. His path to Buck took him within a few feet of Bandit's head. The whites of the horse's eyes were showing as the stranger approached. Bandit suddenly threw his head up and issued a warning snort. Durrell halted immediately, suddenly aware of how close he was to a strange stallion. His attention was on the horse, when Heeley took a step back and whipped around in a fast turn.

'Hold it!' Durrell yelled, moving in to lash out a blow with the butt of the gun.

The stallion moved even faster. His head shot out and his teeth closed on the shoulder of Durrell's coat. The bounty hunter yelled in surprise, pulling himself away and trying to fend off a blow from Heeley. The stallion released his grip and reared, striking out with his powerful legs. One caught Durrell in the chest and knocked him backwards. The bounty hunter landed half on his back and kept rolling. He was gasping for breath, the wind almost knocked out of him, but he couldn't feel the stabbing pain of a broken rib. He struggled to a crouching position, still holding his gun.

Heeley had caught Bandit's reins and was trying to mount his excited horse. Durrell fired once and saw Heeley jerk, crying out as he fell away from the saddle. The stallion half-reared at the gunshot, pulling his reins loose. Durrell stood up, watching the horse more than its owner. Heeley was on the ground, his hand pressed against his side as he tried to crawl to some cover. The stallion snorted, ears pressed flat against its neck as it stared at the bounty hunter. Durrell made a quick decision. He didn't want to shoot such a fine animal, even if Clayton hadn't wanted it for himself, but there was no choice. He couldn't tell how badly hurt Heeley was and there was no time to fetch the rope on his own saddle. He started to raise his gun.

A shot ricocheted off the rock wall behind Durrell's head. He dodged away instinctively, even before he knew where it had come from. A moment later, he identified the gunshot as coming from a Spencer; Beaumont had joined in.

'Goddamn it,' Durrell muttered to himself. He crouched beside a fold of rock and peered back up the shallow canyon. He couldn't see Beaumont but there were plenty of places further up the trail where he could have climbed to overlook this spot. Heeley was still half-curled up on the open ground. Durrell knew that shock would be setting in and he would be really feeling the pain now. Only ten feet of ground separated them. That and the stallion. Durrell gritted his teeth. This was a bad position, but he wanted to take at least one prisoner back to Clayton. Unholstering his second revolver, Durrell suddenly burst into view.

He fired a wild volley of shots with both hands, aiming one set towards Beaumont's likely position, and the other roughly towards the horse. At least one shot grazed the stallion, which squealed and fled back up the trail away from the noise and pain. Durrell ran towards Heeley, pushing the left Smith & Wesson back into its holster as he intended to grab the injured man's shirt. A rifle shot tore the hat from Durrell's head. He ducked, then turned as another shot grazed his arm. He paused to loose another shot towards the hidden rifleman but Beaumont fired back. The bullet cracked past Durrell's ear. He ran, zigzagging towards cover, and finished with a wild dive into a clump of shrubby juniper and tamarisks. They crackled underneath him, filling his nose with their aromatic scent as he crashed through. Plant splinters jabbed into his face as he rolled, then Durrell fell.

The plants had concealed a shallow water-course, dry now. Jonah Durrell dropped a couple of feet and landed in the sandy bed. A couple more shots crashed through the scrubby plants fringing the creek bed, passing above him. Durrell lay still, aware that his guns were almost empty. He had reloads in his pockets, of course, and considered them as he assessed the situation. His right arm was throbbing violently and he could feel the warm trickle of blood under his sleeve. Scratches from the shrubs stung his face and even his legs, where his trousers had got torn. Worse was the dull, aching pain in the middle of his chest where the stallion's hoof had struck. Every gasping breath hurt and Durrell knew he was going to have a massive bruise there for weeks. His face twisted in a wry version of his usual lovely smile. It could have been far worse, and he knew it. As long as Scott Beaumont stayed hidden out there somewhere with a rifle, there was no way Durrell could get to Heeley without coming under fire. He could try drawing shots until Beaumont ran out of bullets, but he didn't know how many the other man carried.

No doubt Billy Hargreaves had heard the shooting and would be on his way across even now. Jonah Durrell was happy to put practicality above vanity and abandoned his hopes of capturing the fugitives alone. He started to reload his guns, waiting for his back-up to arrive.

Scott didn't know whether he'd hit the bounty hunter or not. He'd almost panicked when the dandy-dressed man had burst out, both guns blazing, and charged for Buck. Scott had fired back without thinking and now he was out of bullets. He decided to take the risk and withdrew the steel tube from the rifle's stock to refill it. His last seven bullets filled the tube. When they ran out, there were no more. Scott shoved the tube home and cocked the side hammer before peering around the reddish sandstone rock he was using for cover. He couldn't see the bounty hunter but Buck's legs were still in sight. The rest of him was hidden by the feeble cover of tamarisks and rabbitbush. Scott tugged absently on one of his corkscrew curls as he thought.

His pinto was a few yards back up the trail. A shoe had come loose which was why he had dropped back, leaving Buck to blaze the trail. Scott waited a few moments, then rose and made his way down the trail, dashing from cover to cover and glancing frequently at the bushes where the bounty hunter had disappeared. He reached Buck in less than a minute, leaning over his friend as he continued to dart nervous glances around.

'Buck? Can you move?' he hissed.

Buck was curled on one side, his right hand pressed against his side. His tanned skin was greyish and his eyes glazed with pain. 'Just about.'

Keeping the rifle in his right hand, Scott extended his left arm through the rabbitbush to his friend. 'We need to move before he comes back,' Scott urged. When Buck grabbed his hand, Scott hauled him upright.

Buck gasped, clinging to his friend with his head bowed. Scott's mouth narrowed to a thin line as he listened to his friend's painful breathing. As soon as Buck lifted his head again, Scott slipped his left arm around his waist and helped him away. Buck leaned heavily against him, every step forcing grunts of pain.

'We'll make it,' Scott reassured him, taking more

of his friend's weight. 'Splash's close by and Bandit won't have gone far.'

'He'll come . . . when I whistle,' Buck gasped. He stumbled, only saved from falling by Scott's quick grab.

Scott winced at Buck's gasp of pain at being grabbed but made himself hang on. He could feel the warm dampness of Buck's blood on his own shirt as he supported his friend and tried to keep moving. He forced his way up the winding trail, breathlessly cursing the loose stones that slipped under his feet as he struggled with his burden. They were out of sight of the place where Buck had been ambushed but Scott still hurried, using the butt of the Spencer as a walking-stick on the sloping trail.

Jonah Durrell could faintly hear speech from up on the trail. It was soon drowned by noises from somewhere closer. He tensed into alertness, his dark eyes wide like a feral animal's as he stretched his senses. The sounds were quiet but too noisy to be a wild animal; someone was approaching up the sandy creek-bed. Durrell rose gracefully to his feet and moved in a half crouch, both guns at the ready even though he was sure it was Billy Hargreaves he could hear approaching. They met at the bend of the creek bed.

Hargreaves quickly assessed the bounty hunter's state, noting the patch of dark blood on his sleeve. 'Did they get away?' he hissed angrily.

'I've winged Henley,' Durrell answered succinctly. 'Beaumont's on the trail with him, getting him back to their mounts, I guess.'

Hargreaves glanced again at the shallow wound on Durrell's arm. 'I ain't scared of a schoolteacher and a storekeeper half-breed.' He pushed past the bounty hunter and made his way quickly up the creek bed, the Colt already in his hand.

'Go careful,' Durrell warned, following close. 'Beaumont's useful with that Spencer and he'll use it.'

'You've never heard him talk,' Billy Hargreaves answered. 'He's all hot air and fancy book-learning; he ain't got the grit for a real fight.'

'Fool, how do you think I got this bullet graze . . . ?' Durrell gave up his warning as Billy Hargreaves pushed through the bushes and climbed on to the trail. He followed, guns ready, and stoically ignored the thorns that tore at his already ripped clothes.

Hargreaves paused at the edge of the open trail, his eyes sweeping the ground.

'Look!' he hissed, excitement colouring his voice. He strode forward to the bushes where Buck had taken cover. 'You put lead in him all right.' He rubbed at the fresh patch of blood with the toe of his boot.

Durrell already knew that. He kept a few paces behind, all too aware of the cover this terrain offered to an ambusher. Hargreaves studied the tracks in the soft ground. 'Scott's helping him, look at the way Buck's dragging his feet. Scott must have his hands plumb full.' He bounded eagerly up the trail.

'Careful!' Durrell warned again but his advice was unheeded. He followed, watching rocks and bushes ahead rather than the immediate trail. Hargreaves was moving faster than was sensible but Durrell stuck close behind him, unwilling to let him blunder into trouble unsupported. In the event, it happened very quickly.

Billy Hargreaves rounded a rock to find Scott helping Buck into the pinto's saddle.

'Got you!' he yelled, lifting his guns.

Scott didn't hesitate. Letting go of his friend, he spun and whipped the heavy old rifle to waist height. He fired from instinctive alignment then worked the lever and thumbed back the hammer without pausing to see the effect of his shot.

Billy Hargreaves staggered backwards and fell sprawling, a hole torn through his chest. Jonah Durrell ducked back into the cover of the rock, shaking his head. He heard a horse moving away and stuck his head out for a quick look. He just glimpsed the pinto moving away with a rider slumped awkwardly in the saddle, before another shot from the Spencer grazed the rock just above his head. Back in cover, he could still see Billy Hargreaves, who moaned as he struggled for breath.

'Fool,' Durrell muttered, sorrow showing in his eyes.

Billy focused on him. 'I can't move,' he moaned. 'Did something hit me?'

Durrell ventured another cautious peek around the rock. Beaumont had left; he couldn't be far ahead and he was slowed by his injured friend, but Durrell made no attempt to chase him. Instead, he holstered his left revolver and knelt by the dying young man. He took off his jacket and wadded it up to slip under Billy's head, helping him breathe more easily. Bright blood bubbled from Billy's nose and mouth.

'I'm cold,' he whispered, his eyes wide open. 'Are you there? I can't see too good.'

'I'm with you,' Durrell reassured him, resting one hand on Billy's shoulder. 'I'll stay here.' He settled himself to comfort Billy for the few minutes of life he had left.

The church bell was ringing, calling its single note over and over as Scott rode into Navajo Rock from the south. The town was cloaked in a gentle Sabbath peace. The soft hoof beats of the pinto gelding seemed loud to Scott as he rode, his eyes searching the porches and doors for any danger. Buck needed help. Scott had bound the wound and left him resting, hidden safely, but they needed help. He hadn't told Buck what he intended to do. The stores were all quiet, even the cantina seemed to be closed. Scott noticed that the broken window in Heeley's store had not been fixed yet. The only things moving were a couple of horses tethered to the rails outside the whitewashed church. Taking a deep breath, Scott hitched his pinto outside and walked straight into the wooden porch. Almost every pew was full, the townsfolk listening attentively to Scott's father as he preached. Scott didn't look right or left; he walked up the nave, his boots thumping on the wooden floor. Preacher George fell silent, his eyes fixed upon his dishevelled, dirty son as he approached. Scott's curly hair was wilder than ever and he sported a

matching gingery beard like some old-time prospec-
tor. He stopped level with the front pew, aware of his
ma and sisters sitting almost close enough to touch.

'I've come to ask your forgiveness for Buck. He's
hurt and he needs aid.' The words fell heavily into
the silence.

Preacher George said nothing at first, too
outraged to think. Then his face flushed dark. 'You
want my forgiveness for a murderer?'

'Buck didn't shoot anyone. I killed John Clayton
to save Buck's life!'

'You are a murderer; a lawbreaker. You have
wandered astray and sold your souls to the Devil! You
shall thirst and hunger as you wander through the
desert—'

'Father!' Scott interrupted his father for the first
time in his life. He took a deep breath, then continued. 'Buck needs help; he needs you to be the Good
Samaritan.'

'You are sinners and you shall suffer for your
crimes in the sight of God.'

'Peter Clayton's bounty hunter shot him!'

There was a murmur among the congregation.
Scott ignored them. 'Father, I beg you . . .'

'You are not my son!' Preacher George threw his
hands out as if to cast away his child.

'God is my father!' Scott yelled back. 'Show us the
forgiveness that the Bible tells us about. Help those
in trouble and need. In the name of God, help
Buck!'

The preacher's face flushed even darker. His
fingers gripped the leather-bound Bible in front of

him as if he wanted to pick it up and throw it. 'Do not use the Lord's name, O sinner,' he breathed. 'To come into this sacred place and abuse His name so foully is a crime unto Heaven. You shall burn in the Hellfire for eternity.'

'And so shall you!' Scott pointed at his father. The faint whispers among the congregation died out completely. 'You have no gentleness, no mercy, no kindness. You beat your own children, even your daughters. You gave us the rod instead of love. You denied us all comforts and pleasures and claimed it was for the honour of God. You are unfit to preach the word of God!' A weight seemed to lift from his shoulders as he flung out the accusations he had harboured for so long. Scott swallowed, staring unwaveringly at the preacher. For a moment, there was a sensation of victory, but it faded. Suddenly full of revulsion, Scott turned and strode back through the church.

There was a sudden movement of someone standing in one of the pews. It was Tom Heeley; his daughters and the rest of the townsfolk stared at him.

'Come with me,' he said to Scott. 'I shall help my son.'

No more was said; they left the church together.

ELEVEN

Heeley snatched tins from the shelves of his store, stuffing them into a saddle-bag as he talked. 'Mae baked some biscuits this morning, you can have them too.' He pushed a can into place and hefted the bag, feeling its weight. Slinging it over his shoulder, he crossed to another shelf and took down boxes of bullets. 'I'll fetch you a Winchester, one of the new models.'

'I've got myself a Spencer,' Scott said quietly, rolling a new bedroll around some clothes. Heeley was giving them everything they needed to survive in the desert country. His own father had given them nothing but damnation.

'I've got some shells for that somewhere.' Heeley fastened the buckle of the saddle-bag, pulling it straight and tucking the end into the keeper. 'I want to see him; I want to see my boy and I can't.' He turned to Scott, his eyes full of pain. 'Everyone knows I'm helping you but I got to think of Mae, too. She's got no ma now; I can't leave her without a pa.'

'Buck'll understand. What you're giving us now is plenty.'

'It's not the same as taking care of him myself.'

Scott looked up from tying a pigging thong and caught a glimpse of movement in the rear door. He just saw Mae ducking back out of sight.

'Buck is worried enough about causing trouble for you,' he said. 'He sure as hell doesn't want more.'

'I reckon so.' Heeley crossed to a glass case, opened it and took out some Navajo jewellery. He removed two squash-blossom necklaces, a turquoise-set bracelet and a sandcast belt buckle. Laying them on a piece of cloth, he spoke to Scott as he wrapped them carefully. 'This pawn belongs to Billy Mortimer. I want to offer it to him as a gift.'

Billy Mortimer was Buck's half-Navajo uncle. Scott had only met him a few times but he knew at once that he would help. Among Navajo, nothing was more important than helping relatives.

'I'll find him,' Scott said.

Heeley told him where Billy Mortimer's summer sheep-camp was; and coached him in the basic Navajo greeting. Scott listened carefully, repeating the guttural phrases. He wanted longer to practise but there was no time.

'I'll go fix these to my saddle,' he said, lifting the bedrolls.

John Heeley just nodded.

Scott hadn't travelled far when he heard a horse being ridden at a fast pace behind him. He rode off the trail and got the Spencer out, flipping the lever and thumbing back the side hammer. He was never more surprised than when he saw the rider. It was his sister, Sukie, riding astride their father's horse with her long skirts hitched up so her boots and petticoats showed below the flounces. One hand was grasping the horn of Paul's old saddle as she pulled clumsily on the reins to make her horse stop.

'What in hell are you doing here?' Scott exclaimed, riding into full view.

'I've come to help you and Buck.' She glared at him defiantly.

'You can't do that! Father'll half-kill you.'

'What you said about him is all true. I don't care what he says any more; I want to help you both.' Her face was pale but her voice never wavered.

'For the Lord's sake, Sukie, you're a young lady. You can't just ride off out with men.'

'I can and I have,' she answered. 'You can't go fetch Buck's uncle and look after Buck at the same time. I'll stop and keep camp for him. I can cook and make much better coffee than you anyway,' she added with a typical air.

'How do you know about what I'm planning?' Scott asked anxiously.

'Mae overheard and told me.'

Scott's head reeled at the thought of two girls taking matters into their own hands like this. Young women weren't supposed to defy family and law and plot behind people's backs. On the other hand, he couldn't help admiring his sister's spirit.

'Think about it and go home, Sukie,' he said more gently. 'Ma'll be plumb worried about you.'

'Ma's still got Ruth and Lizzie to worry about. And Father. You set the whole town on its ear with what you said. Ma was saying we'll have to move away and

I don't want to leave Navajo Rock.' Sukie brushed a stray lock of hair back behind her ear. Scott remembered how much she had longed to wear jangling earrings like the Mexican girls in town. Father had forbidden it, of course, lecturing her on the sin of vanity.

Scott's mouth drew into a thin line. 'I'm sorry. I'm real sorry for what I've done to you and Ma.' He smiled involuntarily. 'For there is no friend like a sister in calm or stormy weather,' he quoted. 'She must have been writing about you, Sukie. You're worth more than the rest of my family put together.'

Sukie blushed a dainty pink and took the chance to ride her borrowed horse next to Scott's. 'Then I'm going to keep camp for you?'

Scott shook his heal resignedly. 'I don't reckon I get any choice.'

'You don't.'

Some instinct told Sukie that Buck was awake again. She poured hot water into a tin mug and added some herbs, stirring it up thoroughly. When it had steeped to her satisfaction, she carried it across to where Buck lay wrapped in his bedroll. His face was lightly dewed with sweat and his eyes were unnaturally bright as he watched her.

'How do you feel now?' she asked gently.

'A little better but it still hurts,' he admitted.

The bullet wound had brought on a fever. Buck had been shy at first about letting Sukie clean and bandage the wound, but necessity had overcome modesty. Scott had been gone three days and Buck had been getting sicker on each one. He dozed most of the time now and Sukie watched him, praying for her brother to return. In spite of her worry, she was happy as she tended Buck, and simply watched him as he dozed, glad of the opportunity to look at him for as long as she liked.

'Drink this,' she ordered sweetly, holding the mug out.

He put one hand on hers to guide it; she could feel the trembling of weakness in his arm. Buck obediently drank the potion, used to the bitter taste by now.

'Thanks,' he whispered. He hitched himself upon his elbows while Sukie rearranged the pile of clothes that passed for a pillow, but was glad to lie down again.

'You just rest. Scott'll be back real soon,' Sukie said soothingly. She picked a stray lock of dark brown hair from his face but resisted the temptation to fuss him more. Instead, Sukie unfastened her own hair and began combing it out while she sang the same lullabies that she had sung to her younger sisters. Buck relaxed and gradually drifted back to sleep.

Hoof beats disturbed the camp shortly after dawn. Sukie untangled herself from her blanket, fastening the front of her crumpled cotton dress with one hand as she reached for Buck's Winchester with the other. Her heart thumped wildly.

'Sukie?' It was her brother's voice at last.

'Oh, Scott.' She put down the rifle and finished arranging her dress.

He rode around the curve of the arroyo with a

stranger beside him. Sukie recognized Buck's uncle; a tall, lean-boned man with his long hair worn in the traditional bun. He dismounted, leaving Scott to tend the horses, and Sukie joined him as he crouched beside Buck. She had always been rather afraid of Buck's Navajo relatives, but she knelt beside Billy Mortimer without fear as he gently examined his nephew, his long fingers sensitive to Buck's pain.

'The bullet will have to come out,' Billy Mortimer said, his voice tinged with breathy Navajo gutturals. 'Make hot water,' he ordered.

The operation was necessarily brutal but Sukie stayed until it was over. 'You must go home now,' Scott told her afterwards as she wound her sun-roughened hair into a thick braid. 'We'll stay at Billy Mortimer's place awhile until Buck is better. His wife'll look after Buck.' He touched his sister's hair gently.

'I'll go stay with Mae,' Sukie answered matter-of-factly. She had left home without a bonnet and the sun had turned her face and nose red. 'Mr Heeley won't mind.'

Scott nodded approvingly. 'You must go see Ma some time. She'll have worried her heart out over you, even if Father don't want to see either of us again.'

'All right.' Sukie stood on tiptoe to kiss her brother's cheek.

He held her horse as she hitched up her dress and mounted. 'For ever, and for ever, farewell,' he declaimed dramatically. 'If we do meet again, why we shall smile! If not, why then, this parting was well made.'

Sukie laughed a little sadly, then glanced once at Buck and rode away.

Scott and Buck sat on the ground and watched as Billy Mortimer hammered the silver. It was Mexican silver, almost pure, soft and easy to work. The anvil was no more than a simple piece of iron but it served as he skilfully eased the lump into a bar. Under repeated, light strokes, the bar would become a bracelet, but as yet the design was locked away in the mind of Buck's uncle. He had seen it clearly, even before he'd touched the silver, but the young men watched and waited to see how it would come out.

'You hammer a little while,' Billy told Buck. He gave his nephew the hammer and moved away, letting Buck seat himself comfortably at the anvil.

The sounds of the camp hummed quietly around them during the interval. Behind them was the steady rattle and clack of the looms as the women did their weaving. A shaggy dog lay stretched in the dust, panting in the late September heat. They had been here over a month as Buck recovered from his injury. Both young men had slipped into the Navajo way, rising at dawn, living under the sky, sharing the life with the close-knit family. Scott kept the children amused with his clumsy attempts to learn Navajo and asking endless questions about things they thought only a baby didn't know.

Buck's first strokes on the silver were hesitant but he settled into a steady rhythm as he warmed to the work. He had been practising for a week now, learning to make the metal bend to his will. Billy Mortimer watched a few moments, then began hammering out coins into conchos. His equipment was simple; the iron anvil, a hard wooden board with depressions for shaping bosses and beads, dies made from iron files. It produced beautiful jewellery though, pure Navajo in taste in spite of his white blood.

The calm of the work was interrupted by a shout. The three men looked up and saw Singing Boy, Billy's second son, running along the narrow trail that led down the slope into this little valley. As they looked up, he waved his arms and yelled again, all the time racing across the rough ground as gracefully as an antelope.

'What's he saying?' Scott asked urgently. He dropped the braided rope he'd been fiddling with.

Singing Boy paused for a moment to shout a couple of sentences. Billy Mortimer rose at once. 'Four white men are coming here. One he thinks is the father of that man who was killed, and one is the white-man preacher; your father,' he added to Scott.

'What's your father doing here?' Buck asked stupidly, looking up as Scott scrambled to his feet.

'I asked him for help and he condemned us both to hell,' Scott admitted. 'He's realized where we might be and sold us out to Clayton and the hunter.' His freckled face flushed red with anger.

Preacher George travelled out amongst the Navajo now and again, trying to convert them to Christianity. Buck's uncle had been a particular target for his crusade and the preacher knew where his pastures were.

Buck stood up too, swearing.

'I'll keep them here if I can,' Billy Mortimer promised. He switched to Navajo to shout orders to his wife and family.

As Buck and Scott saddled their horses, others gathered their belongings and added what little food they could spare. They were ready to go in less than three minutes. Singing Boy arrived in camp almost breathless and described the other two men with the preacher. One was obviously the bounty hunter and the other was one of Clayton's men, probably Oscar Crawford.

Billy Mortimer grinned. 'The preacher will find I remember less English than I did,' he promised. 'I will tell him I sent you away two weeks ago. You are unlucky and I am only a superstitious Navajo.'

A slight smile touched Buck's face. 'Thank you.' It was all he had time to say before he wheeled Bandit around and set the black horse into a gallop, Scott by his side.

A narrow goat-track led over a low rim on the far side of the little valley. The horses raced over it, clearing the rim and plunging down the other side just as the hunters came into sight. A fast escape from the valley had already been planned so there was no need to talk as the fugitives rode. Buck led them down a steep scramble and jumped his horse down into a dry wash. It led them west and curved around a butte. The ground turned to smooth rock and Buck slowed. The horses blew briskly through distended nostrils after the fifteen-minute run.

'You all right?' Scott asked quietly, ducking his head under a cottonwood branch. Buck nodded; he was sitting slightly stiffly in his saddle, aware of dull pain in his side. There was nothing to do but keep going and hope that the hunters would lose their trail on the rock.

They left the wash up a talus slope, the horses walking with lowered heads as they picked their way over the loose stones. From there they skirted the rim of another valley and pushed the horses over a flat stretch of mesa before plunging down into another series of washes and draws. Grey clouds had built over Black Mesa and were drifting easterly towards them. Buck could smell the faint perfume of sagebrush on the cold breeze that blew fitfully. His heart rose at the thought of rain, even as he ran for his life. He was hurting more when they pulled up in a narrow draw. He dismounted awkwardly, staggering for a moment until he caught his balance. Scott was already climbing to a narrow ridge that overlooked the whole of the mesa they were on. They waited together, lying flat and sheltered by thin scrub so they couldn't be seen. Buck's breath had finally slowed when four riders came into view on the far side of the mesa.

'When troubles come, they come not single spies but in battalions,' Scott quoted.

'Shakespeare. He tracked us over the rock,' Buck said, watching their chasers. 'That hunter's damned good.' The man on the grey horse rode in front, studying the ground as he led the others on.

'And Father will tell him about all the other camps we could go to,' Scott said. 'We've got to shake them off.'

They remounted and rode on, but every time they looked back, the hunters were a little closer. Bandit and the pinto were out of condition and couldn't keep up the steady pace of grain-fed horses. The strain was beginning to tell on Buck too, who sat unevenly in his saddle. Above them, the sky grew darker as clouds built up. The air grew cooler, with fitful breezes until, suddenly, the downpour began. A dry, stale smell rose from the ground and was swiftly washed away in the scent of sagebrush and earth. Buck lifted his face, letting the heavy rain pour over his skin.

'We got to take shelter,' Scott called above the hammering of the rain.

'Sure,' Buck answered happily, his heart lifted by the rain.

It was getting difficult to see anything much through the pouring water. The horses moved reluctantly, their heads close to their chests, and their tails clamped down. They rode on for another fifteen minutes before Scott gave a cry of triumph.

'There! Our shelter from the stormy blast!' He pointed at the dim shape of a Navajo hogan.

Buck rode up to it with him, and soon felt that something was wrong. The sheep pens were empty, there were no horses or dogs around and no smell of wet dung. He nudged Bandit around to the north and saw the hole knocked through the wall.

'We can't go in there,' he called to Scott who had already dismounted.

'Whyever not?' Scott answered. His hat gave his face some protection from the rain, but his clothes were streaming with water.

'It's a ghost hogan. Someone died in there,' Buck answered, wiping rain away from his eyes. His side hurt and he was tired enough to lean on his saddle horn.

'If it's abandoned, so much the better,' Scott said. 'We can take the horses inside.' Buck shook his head stubbornly. 'We're plumb soaked already. Let's ride on.'

'You need a rest and so do the horses. Let's stop and brew coffee. They can't be tracking us through this.'

'It's haunted,' Buck insisted.

Scott bit back a sharp answer. 'That's a Navajo superstition,' he pointed out, trying to sound reasonable. 'It's a pagan idea. You're Christian, remember, like your mother.'

Buck scowled but he understood what his friend was saying. He peered through the heavy rain at the hogan, balancing his deep fears against the everyday common sense of the whitewashed church. His mother wouldn't have hesitated to enter the hogan, serene in her belief in God. Buck slithered down from his saddle and led Bandit inside the hogan without stopping to think.

It took over an hour for the heavy rain to ease off. Scott stepped outside for a few moments.

'There's no sign of anyone. I bet they holed up for shelter someplace and this rain's washed out our tracks. We can move on.'

Buck stood up and joined him in the doorway. He hadn't spoken much while they sheltered but there was a new calmness in his face.

'I won't let that son-of-a-bitch drive me from my home,' he said. 'I'm through running from Clayton.'

'He's got that bounty hunter with him,' Scott reminded him.

'That bounty hunter doesn't want to kill us, he just wants his reward. I know you didn't set out to kill John Clayton, but we can't go home until we kill Peter Clayton.'

'I was a fool to kill John Clayton,' Scott said.

'He would have killed me if you hadn't,' Buck answered. 'You were justified.'

'I guess Peter Clayton's got a right to hate us but that doesn't give him the right to lynch us and to set a bounty killer on us,' Scott said slowly.

It was as hard for him to think of deliberately killing a man as it had been for Buck to enter the ghost hogan.

'I want to go home again,' Buck said, looking at his friend. 'The only person stopping me is Peter Clayton.'

'What are you aiming to do?' Scott asked.

Buck turned to look at the rain-washed desert. 'We'll find them, and set them an ambush.'

TWELVE

'Where?' Scott asked as they led the horses outside.

'Navajo Rock; our fort. We can put the horses out of sight and jump them from above while they're sat in the dead end.'

'That sounds smart enough. Let's go look for them,' Scott said.

The two fugitives had to ride for nearly half an hour before finding their pursuers. Buck rode boldly on to a rim overlooking a shallow valley and scanned the ground below.

'That's them,' he said simply, pointing to the four mounted figures below.

One of the horsemen saw him against the sky and pointed, calling to the others. Clayton turned his horse first, spurring it into a gallop as he headed straight towards Buck. Buck stayed where he was a moment longer, then moved away.

'They're about twenty minutes behind us,' he told Scott.

'We should be able to stay ahead until we reach

the rock,' Scott answered. 'We don't want them to get
close enough to start throwing lead.'

They rode on, no longer needing to talk.

Navajo Rock itself was a butte adjoining the mesa
to the north and east of the town. The two of them
had climbed and ridden all over the mesa as boys.
Their fort was a secret place that Buck had discov-
ered one day. When they reached the rock, Buck
turned his horse along the narrow cut through the
sandstone rock. The afternoon sun gilded the upper
reaches of the walls that surrounded them, but the
bottom of the cut was in cool shade, welcome after
their long run across country.

'I'm sure glad I never told Father about this,' Scott
said. He had shared few of his secrets and games with
his father.

'Or John Clayton. He never did find it, did he?'
Buck grinned as he remembered how annoyed John
had been at not being able to uncover their secret for
himself.

The cut seemed to end in a solid wall of stone.
Juniper hid the lower part of the dead end, but the
banded rock rose above the shrub, cutting off any
escape. Buck dismounted and hooked his stirrups over
his saddle horn before leading his horse forward.
Bandit ducked his head, following obediently through
the aromatic bushes. Only when amongst the juniper
and almost nose to nose with the rock beyond, was the
secret revealed. The juniper hid a narrow window
eroded through the sandstone wall at the end of the
cut. The window was just wide enough for the stallion
to squeeze through. The fenders on Buck's saddle

scraped against the sides of the window. He inspected the damage as Scott led the pinto through. On the far side was their fort: a short extension to the cut with no other way out except back through the window.

'We can't run from here,' Buck said, loosening the stallion's cinch.

'His flight was madness: when our actions do not, our fears do make us traitors,' Scott quoted. 'I sure as all hell didn't *murder* anybody and I'm through with acting like I did. Peter Clayton's got to see reason.'

Buck nodded, and held out his hand. 'We got into this because you were trying to help me. You've been a good pal.'

They shook hands, then set about getting ready to meet their pursuers.

They would hear them coming before they could see them. Buck and Scott had climbed the wall above the window and flattened themselves into hiding places overlooking the end of the narrow canyon. They stayed low as the four riders came into view, riding single file along the cut into its dead end. Jonah Durrell was leading, a gun in his hand, while Peter Clayton pressed his horse close behind. Durrell saw the apparently solid wall at the end of the cut and reined in, looking around.

'Where in hell are they?' Peter Clayton demanded as Preacher George and Oscar Crawford rode in behind them.

The end of the cut was just wide enough for them to mill together. All four had ridden hard but Durrell somehow looked fresher and cleaner than the other trail-weary men.

'You've taken the wrong damned trail,' Peter Clayton accused.

Durrell shook his head, unperturbed by the rancher's anger. 'They came this way for sure.'

'Well then, where in the blue blazes. . . ?'

'We're here!' Scott had shifted carefully to his feet.

Buck did the same and they stood on the narrow rock, above the mounted men, holding guns trained steadily on their enemies. Both Peter Clayton and Preacher George flushed with anger, their eyes cold with hate. Jonah Durrell grimaced briefly, annoyed with himself for walking into a trap, then prepared himself to wait. He brushed some fine trail-dust from his coat and settled his hat evenly. Oscar Crawford took his cue from his boss.

'What do you want, you yellow bastards?' called Clayton. The rancher's fine clothes were wrinkled and coated in dust. He ached from the long ride after his son's killers but he sat upright in the saddle, his hate lending him strength.

'I want you to see reason,' Scott answered. He could see his father's lips moving and guessed that the preacher was praying under his breath.

'You murdered my son,' Clayton spat.

'Your son was trying to murder me!' Buck yelled. 'It was his gun and he drew iron to try and plug me!'

'You shot him and I'm going to see you swing for it, 'breed!'

Buck took a sharp breath, trying to calm himself. 'Drop your guns,' he ordered.

While Clayton shouted an angry answer, Durrell leaned sideways to let the Smith & Wesson he was holding drop gently to the ground.

'What are you doing?' Crawford exclaimed. The red-haired cowboy pushed his horse past the preacher's to confront the hunter.

'I'm doing like the man with the gun pointed at me told me to do,' Durrell answered, unworried by Crawford's anger.

'I hired you to fight!' Clayton snapped.

'You didn't hire me to get killed like a raw fool,' Durrell answered.

'Drop your other iron,' Buck called down. 'And you, Clayton.'

The rancher turned his attention to the young man he hated. 'I don't take orders from no squaw boy.'

Buck fired a single shot over the rancher's head. The crack echoed around the enclosed space, spooking the horses. In the confusion, Preacher George moved his horse close to Crawford's side.

'When I give an order, you do it or I'll shoot,' Buck yelled, his voice harsh with rage. 'Drop your goddamned guns!'

As Peter Clayton yelled abuse back at Buck, Preacher George snatched the gun from Crawford's belt and fired a quick shot at his son.

Scott felt a sudden, hot pain in his shoulder even as he saw the action. He jerked sideways and lost his balance on the narrow stone ridge he was standing on. With a yell of pain and surprise, he fell to a sitting position and began to slide towards the twenty-foot drop. In spite of the shock, he managed to keep hold of the gun that Buck's father had given him.

'He who spareth the rod, hateth his child,' quoted the preacher, his voice ringing above the confusion that exploded around him. 'You have sinned in the eyes of the Lord, who gave up His only son that you might be saved.' The last words were drowned in the crackle of gunfire.

Buck was as surprised at the first shot as Scott was. He turned towards his friend, momentarily forgetting the danger from the men below. He realized his mistake almost at once, turning back so fast he almost lost his own footing. Durrell was drawing his other Smith & Wesson and Peter Clayton had snatched for his Colt. A wild shot from the rancher cracked past Buck's ear, making him shake his head as he ducked away. He crouched behind the bulge of rock he'd used as a hiding-place, firing back down into the canyon. His first shot struck Oscar Crawford, almost knocking him from his horse. The cowhand screamed in agony, clutching at the wound in his belly. Buck ignored the sound, intent on getting the rancher in his sights.

Scott's toes hit a ridge in the rock and his slide halted. He was lying flat, his already grubby shirt torn and rucked up under his back and blood seeping from a painful bullet graze across his left shoulder. He sucked in a deep breath, too shocked and scared to act for the moment. The screaming from below jerked him back to reality. He glanced about, aware of his exposed position. To his left, there was a shelf of rock with a slight overhang. With a silent prayer, Scott pushed himself over and scrabbled across the sun-warmed rock. Blood dripped from his shoulder, leaving a trail of stains on the golden sandstone.

Buck fired just as a shot hit the rock he was using as cover. Chips of stone flew into his face, momentarily blinding him. He ducked back, shaking his head and wiping his free hand roughly across his face. The stinging pain fuelled his anger. He was hungry and stiff, fed up with being chased around the country and kept from his home. As soon as he could see again, Buck leaned into the open once more. He glimpsed Durrell aiming at him but ignored the hunter. Buck fired straight at Peter Clayton and saw him rock in his saddle, crying out with pain. Buck grinned widely, unaware of having done so. The rancher ducked low in his saddle and tried to manoeuvre his horse behind the bounty hunter's grey. The grey swung around, spoiling Durrell's shot at Buck.

Buck never even noticed the near miss. 'You're acting yellow, Clayton!' he yelled, thumbing back the hammer of his Colt. 'At least John fought and died like a man!'

Peter Clayton straightened at the insult, turning and lifting his gun in one motion. He was scowling and yelling something in return. Buck didn't hear the words, oblivious to all except the rancher's face below the glittering silver conchos on his hat. Buck fired first, exclaiming in fierce delight as Peter Clayton was pitched backwards off his horse. He wanted to fire again but the rancher was hidden from his sight amongst the horses. Buck swore, half standing to try and see Clayton.

Scott scrambled on to the shelf of rock, his heart

thudding with fear. It was narrow enough but felt marvellously secure after lying out on the steep wall above the canyon. The angle of the rock gave him some cover from anyone close to the wall directly below his position but he was still exposed to his father's view. Preacher George stared up at his wayward son, reciting the Lord's Prayer aloud as he aimed.

'Father!' Scott cried. 'This is not justice!'

'It is the Lord's justice,' the preacher replied, firing again.

The angle was an awkward one and the preacher had rarely touched a gun before. Scott flinched as the bullet struck the rock a bare inch from his leg and ricocheted off. The same frustration and bitterness that had led him to denounce his father in the church drove him to act at last.

'Let God take whom He wants,' Scott hissed, firing back at his father.

His heart jumped as the preacher reeled in his saddle, dropping the gun. Scott held his breath, only letting it out when he saw he had hit his father through the shoulder. Preacher George's arm hung by his side as he glared up at his son.

'Finish it then; I am not afraid!' the preacher challenged.

'Neither am I!' Scott yelled, raising his gun again. He gazed at his father along the sights of his gun, then slowly lowered the revolver. 'No. I won't be like you,' he called. 'I will have mercy.' He wasn't sure whether sparing his father's life was mercy or punishment for the preacher, but Scott had finally made his choice to follow his own path in life. His father's opinion could no longer hurt him.

Buck didn't notice the exchange between Scott and his father until it was almost over. He couldn't see Clayton but there was still one threat left. Buck turned his attention to the bounty hunter and saw Durrell holding his hand up, holding his gun by its barrel.

'Don't shoot!' Durrell called. 'You hit Clayton in the head; he's cashed.'

'Drop your iron,' Buck ordered.

Jonah Durrell obeyed carefully. 'If Clayton's dead, there's no one to pay my fee,' he said smiling. 'I only let people shoot at me when I'm paid for it.'

Buck studied the handsome man for a moment. Durrell was alert but relaxed.

'Clayton was the one with the grudge against you,' Durrell continued. 'If I'm not getting paid, I don't give a damn what happens to you.'

Buck couldn't help warming to the hunter's honesty. 'What about your professional pride?' he asked.

Durrell smiled. 'My personal pride tells me I surely look better like this than getting all shot up, especially by some storekeeper. I know you two aren't killers.' He glanced down at where Peter Clayton lay. ' 'Cept when you gets provoked,' he added.

Buck let out a gusty sigh; he could go home now. He looked to see what had happened to Scott.

Back among the familiar smells of the store, Buck hugged his sister, Mae. He lingered against her then detached himself slowly, moved by her lovely smile, so like their mother's. Then he turned to Sukie, standing next to Scott, and disregarded propriety to gather her into a swift hug.

'Thank you,' he said close up, moving away again to look into her brown eyes, wide with amazement and pleasure. 'You treated me better than I deserve.'

Sukie was speechless for once, returning to Scott's side when Buck released her.

Scott glanced at his sister, a grin tugging at the corners of his mouth. 'I appreciate you letting Sukie stay here,' he said to Tom Heeley.

When Preacher George had ridden out to help hunt down his own son, Mrs Beaumont had packed her goods and her two youngest children and moved back to her family in Missouri. Sukie had refused to leave Navajo Rock in spite of her mother's pleas.

'We've enjoyed the company,' Tom Heeley said. 'The house has been mighty quiet these last weeks.' The leathery storekeeper had hardly stopped smiling since Buck and Scott had returned to town.

'You can keep house for me,' Scott suggested to his sister.

Sukie gave a mocking sniff. 'You're only saying that so you won't have to cook any more.'

Scott put on an expression of injured innocence. 'Why, Sukie; that's the meanest . . .'

His protest was interrupted by the jangle of the bell over the door.

Sheriff Millard entered the store, accompanied by Jonah Durrell. Durrell smiled at the two young women as he adjusted the set of his shirt cuffs, finishing the details of his appearance.

The sheriff nodded at Buck and Scott from under his firmly set white Stetson. Before the sheriff could speak, Tom Heeley stepped forward. 'Buck killed Peter Clayton in self-defence.'

'I've gotten a description of what happened from this gent here,' Millard said, indicating Durrell.

'A man that Clayton hired to kill us right after he tried lynching us,' Scott put in.

Millard nodded slowly. 'I know all that. I didn't come here to arrest you.'

There was silence for a moment as Buck, Scott and their families stared at the sheriff.

'There's enough grief in this town already,' Millard told them. 'I don't believe either of you hotheads set out to kill John Clayton; he got shot through his own meanness. His pa broke the law and got even meaner.' The sheriff glanced sideways at Durrell, who seemed completely relaxed and unashamed. 'There's no sense sending anyone to trial for it. I'm going to write it up as self-defence.'

Sukie gave a whoop of happiness and flung her arms around her brother. Scott lifted her clear into the air, grinning all over his freckled face. Buck was too relieved to react; he simply closed his eyes.

'There'll be no trial?' Tom Heeley repeated.

Millard nodded. 'Waste of public money. It's kinder to let things be. 'Sides, there's not another school teacher for a hundred miles and my Billy-Joe's got to get a good education somehow.'

Scott grinned at that but Buck was still thinking of the Claytons.

'What does Mrs Clayton want?' he asked.

'She plans to sell up, move someplace else; start over,' the sheriff answered.

'Did my father say anything?' Scott asked, glancing at Millard and Durrell.

It was the bounty hunter who answered. 'He said it was the Lord's wish for him to minister to the Indians in the north. I guess he was thinking of Dakota territory.'

Scott tugged a ribbon on his sister's golden-yellow dress. 'I guess Ma'll be happier, really. She can have all the cushions and comforts she wants now.'

'Pa always did love God more than he loved us,' Sukie answered.

Millard spoke again. 'I'll leave you folks now. I reckon you'll be wanting to talk.'

'I want to have a hot bath and get some clean clothes on,' Buck said vehemently. He glanced at his sister, Mae, hoping she would offer to fill the copper, and found her staring at the handsome bounty hunter.

Jonah saw Buck's glance. He swept his hat off with a graceful gesture and bowed. 'I'd surely like to make proper acquaintance with two such charming ladies,' he said. 'But you'll be wanting to talk to your brothers.'

'Well ... I'm ...' Mae started to protest and stopped in confusion.

Jonah took her hand and kissed it. 'You are the loveliest little storekeeper I ever saw,' he said gallantly. He bowed again and left, followed by the sheriff.

Mae gazed at the door as it closed after him, evidently overwhelmed. Tom Heeley looked equally stunned at the flattering and forward behaviour towards his daughter.

'Well said: that was laid on with a trowel,' Scott quoted.

Buck let out a shout of laughter at Scott's characteristic habit. The laughter spread as the relief hit them at last. The long nightmare was over. Buck hugged his youngest sister as he gazed around the store, seeing all the familiar packages, barrels and boxes.

'You know what my favourite quotation is?' he asked. 'Home, sweet home.'